THE BILLIONAIRE'S ROCK STAR

THE SUTTON BILLIONAIRES SERIES, BOOK 4

LORI RYAN

OTHER BOOKS BY LORI RYAN

The Sutton Billionaires Series:

The Billionaire Deal

Reuniting with the Billionaire

The Billionaire Op

The Billionaire's Rock Star

The Billionaire's Navy SEAL

Falling for the Billionaire's Daughter

The Sutton Capital Intrigue Series:

Cutthroat

Cut and Run

Cut to the Chase

The Sutton Capital on the Line Series:

Pure Vengeance

Latent Danger

The Triple Play Curse Novellas:

Game Changer

Game Maker

Game Clincher

The Heroes of Evers, TX Series:

Love and Protect

Promise and Protect

Honor and Protect (An Evers, TX Novella)

Serve and Protect

Desire and Protect

Cherish and Protect

Treasure and Protect

The Dark Falls, CO Series:

Dark Falls

Dark Burning

Dark Prison

Coming Soon – The Halo Security Series:

Dulce's Defender

Hannah's Hero

Shay's Shelter

Callie's Cover

Grace's Guardian

Sophie's Sentry

Sienna's Sentinal

For the most current list of Lori's books, visit her website: loriryanromance.com.

ACKNOWLEDGMENTS

I'd like to thank my incredibly supportive husband and my kids for putting up with the madness of deadlines and rewrites. Thank you to my critique group for all of the brainstorming and reading drafts and support. You guys are absolutely fabulous!

Thank you to Patricia Thomas for editing, copyediting, and working with such tight deadlines and turn-arounds. Thank you to Bev Harrison for proofing the original version of this book and my incredibly giving team of early readers for proofing this update book.

Pam, Antje, Carol, Yvonne, Stevi, Linda, Bev S., and anyone I'm forgetting. You guys are incredible! And, thank you to all of my beta readers: Anne, Bette, Dianne, Ashley, and any others I missed. Your input and help is always appreciated more than you can know!

AUTHOR'S NOTE

If you haven't read Jesse and Zach's story, you can grab that by joining my Facebook group here: facebook.com/groups/397438337278006

CHAPTER 1

*P*J Cantrell laughed and waved her arm over her head one more time for the crowd before stepping off the stage. It would take her a few minutes to catch her breath and change into clean clothes, then she would head out to the side stage door to sign autographs.

Meeting with her fans after every show and thanking them for coming out to see her could take an hour or more, but it made the difference between a great concert and an amazing experience they wouldn't forget. That was important to her.

Her tour manager met her backstage and immediately shuffled her toward her dressing room with more urgency than usual. Lydia was always tightly wound, but this was different.

Flanked by Lydia's assistant—who also happened to be Lydia's younger brother—Ellis, and PJ's security detail, Carl and Jeff, it quickly became clear she wouldn't be signing autographs tonight.

"What's going on?" PJ asked, glancing over her shoulder and spotting Ellis's concern as they rushed down the hall, not stopping for any of the people calling out to her.

He wasn't very good at masking his feelings and he looked especially distressed tonight.

"Let's get you to the dressing room first," Lydia murmured as they rounded the corner.

Ellis spoke from behind her. "It'll be all right, PJ. It'll blow over quickly, I'm sure," he said, earning a scowl from Lydia.

The crush Ellis had was one-sided, but he was endearing and completely devoted. PJ had already recognized his importance on her team in the six months he'd been with them, even though an outsider might not see it right away since he often seemed like all he was doing was hanging around like a lovesick lapdog.

"It's Kurt Tolleson," Lydia said as she pressed an iPad into PJ's hands.

PJ groaned and rolled her eyes. "What happened? I thought the media never picked up on the fact he was still dating me when he started dating his groupie?"

Getting over the awful breakup with the lead singer of Visceral Bond last year hadn't been easy. She hadn't been in love with Kurt, so his betrayal had been more humiliating than hurtful, but at least it had stayed quiet at the time.

No one had known he'd actually gone straight from her bed —quite literally—into his groupie's on a routine basis, completely fooling PJ the entire time.

Lydia was talking, but PJ wasn't listening. All she could do was stare at the screen.

"Debra is already working on getting this taken down. By the time you wake up tomorrow, we'll have it spun––" Lydia said.

PJ knew her manager, Debra Manning, would be in her Los Angeles office no matter how late it was, working to handle this for her. It's what she did.

There was no way PJ could pull her eyes off the screen as she watched a reporter read an entry from PJ's journal during an interview with Kurt Tolleson.

Her very private journal that no one should have been able to get their hands on. She heard her words, her embarrassing words about the first time they'd slept together, being read for all the world to hear.

Then her words when she found out about the breakup. How humiliated she'd felt. How ticked off she'd been when the betrayal became apparent.

All of the details about his cheating, how she'd discovered the other woman's underpants in his pocket one night after a show, the way he'd laughed at her when she confronted him, calling her nothing more than a cheap piece of ass he could get anywhere—all of it was laid bare for the world.

She watched as Kurt flushed when they asked him about the 'indiscretion.' So far, the interview didn't seem that bad. At least she came out looking better than him.

But, what really had her panicking was the fact that they had her journal—or, at the very least, parts of it. *This cannot be happening.* PJ swallowed hard and tried to focus on the interview on the screen.

"PJ is a really wonderful girl and is still a good friend," he said to the camera, his arm slung around the same groupie he'd cheated with as he flat-out lied about having any kind of friendship with PJ.

He turned away from the camera and walked off, but the video kept going for several seconds. And then PJ heard it.

A mic somewhere on one of the cameras had picked up his next comment to Erika—the woman he'd left PJ for. It was fuzzy and poor quality, but the words were unmistakable. "A little needy and sort of like screwing a dead fish, but a nice girl."

Embarrassment burned a pit in her chest. She'd been in this business a long time and was used to the constant critiquing and judging being in the spotlight brought with it. It was a part of her life the way driving a car was a part of life for most people.

That didn't mean it stopped hurting.

"I'm sorry, PJ," Ellis was saying.

"Enough, Ellis," Lydia snapped. "She doesn't need you

babying her. All we have to do is spin this. Kurt and his girlfriend will come out of this looking shallow and vain while people see you as a victim of their callousness."

PJ wasn't sure why being a victim was any better here, but she let Lydia talk. She gave a weak smile and nod to Ellis, knowing Lydia's biting ways often hurt him.

The woman was intense and could be difficult to deal with, but she was damn good at her job. She took care of everything for all of them on tour, and they couldn't function without her. They all made concessions because of it.

Ellis and Lydia were both equally as devoted to PJ and her career; they simply acted on that in different ways with their very different personalities.

But, right now PJ couldn't worry about Ellis's feelings. Her mind whirled.

She could handle Kurt's comments. She'd grown a thick skin in this industry, and a few embarrassing words couldn't do very much to damage her.

But that wasn't what had her hands shaking and her chest feeling like someone had it in a vice, twisting the breath from her body. No, it was the knowledge that someone had gotten into her private journal that sent PJ's heart pounding.

Did they have the whole thing? Did they know everything? PJ blinked as she fought back tears. That journal *could not* get out.

She didn't listen to the rest of Lydia's plans as her mind raced back to the last time she'd written in her journal. Two nights ago, and she was absolutely positive she'd put it away when she was finished.

"I'm going back to the hotel," she said as she handed the iPad to Ellis and grabbed her bag. She didn't want to face anyone else. She glanced at her phone and saw several missed calls from her parents.

They might be her parents and she knew they loved her, but they'd already dealt with a lot when she was younger. *Now this?* Hearing about their daughter's sex life in excruciating detail?

No. She didn't want to talk to them right now. And, she needed to find out how bad this was. She needed to know if that journalist had the whole journal or just a piece of it.

Her bodyguards, Carl and Jeff, helped her slip out of the building and bundled her into her car. She sank into the welcoming softness of the leather seat and took a deep breath, bracing herself as Carl shut the door.

He would follow in a large SUV while Jeff sat in the front seat with her driver, Moore. Both men were silent as they pulled out of the secured parking garage and onto the city street. They had to know she was in no mood to talk to anyone after the night's events.

When PJ's career as one of the youngest country singers in the United States—and then one of the biggest crossover pop singers in the world—took off at the age of fifteen, she'd had a short time when she struggled with alcohol addiction and a spiraling private life, but she'd since cleaned herself up.

Now, most people said she handled the spotlight better than a lot of stars. At twenty-nine, she was better equipped to deal with the pressures than she had been at fifteen.

But, tonight had pushed those boundaries. Before the car had gone two blocks, PJ read her journal words on Facebook posts, in tweets, every site she pulled up on her iPhone. Private clips with personal details about their intimate relationship....

PJ's hands shook as she pushed the button to engage the privacy panel between the driver's seat and the passenger area before opening the small Coach bag she carried with her everywhere.

Swiping at her tears, she felt inside the lining of her bag, but she already knew she wouldn't find it. The USB drive, designed to look like a tube of lipstick, was no longer tucked into the tear in the lining of her bag. It was gone.

She closed her eyes and leaned her head back against the cool seat. The precautions she'd taken with the journal should have been enough. She'd never kept her journal on paper, never kept it on her computer or stored it in a cloud drive. It didn't take a genius to know that would have left her open to someone stealing it.

Privacy wasn't something that existed in her world, and she knew the chances of someone finding her journal if she kept it online or on her laptop were too great. But, she never thought anyone would actually find the hidden drive.

Even if someone spotted it, they would have thought it was an old lipstick, and she'd never told anyone it was there.

She'd gotten used to keeping the journal in rehab and had never given up the habit. It was her respite, her outlet for things that couldn't even go into her songs. Things she couldn't tell anyone. And, now it was out there.

She tried not to panic as she thought about all that was in the journal, all of the private details that whoever had taken it would be able to sell. Lord knows, they'd probably made a ton selling the entries about Kurt to JMZ's *Celebrity News*, the station that seemed to be the originating point for the Kurt Tolleson interview tonight.

How much would they get for selling it? And, did she have any hope of getting it back before they did?

PJ swiped at the rest of her tears, hoping her mascara wasn't running down her cheeks. She gazed out the window at the traffic that kept the town car moving at a crawl as it made its way to her hotel. She'd have to call soon. It was time to warn her Aunt Susie and Uncle Brian about what might be released. They would need to be prepared.

CHAPTER 2

*G*abe Sawyer was in as foul a mood as he'd ever been. He stared out the floor-to-ceiling windows that lined one wall of his hotel suite, providing a view of the New York City skyline that was just one of the things that made his hotels famous.

The opulence that surrounded him was nothing but the best —furnishings with rich fabrics and textures that screamed lavish and wrapped visitors in luxury and comfort. The off-white tones with deep garnet and orange accents added to the beauty of the room and matched the flowers that graced vases strategically placed throughout the suite.

His cell phone rang, drawing his attention away from the ice cubes melting in the glass of whiskey on the glass end table beside him.

Caller ID showed *Jack Sutton* was calling....

Gabe and Jack had been friends for years, and he was one of the few people Gabe talked to when he was in the kind of mood he was in tonight. They'd talked a lot lately, trying to figure out the next direction Gabe should take with his Grand Hotels line.

He'd built his luxury line of hotels eighteen years ago, with a large chunk of the start-up money coming from Sutton Capital, Jack's company.

Grand Towers was his most elite line of five-star hotels with locations across the country and around the globe. Each hotel had dual towers with luxury penthouse suites in the ten-thousand-dollar per night range. He stood in one now and watched the New York skyline through his window.

After he'd made his name with the Towers, he'd ventured into executive suites for long-term stays, creating Grand Garden Suites. This was followed shortly after with Family Grand Hotels —a chain targeting families with budget-friendly pricing and family-focused destinations.

And now, he was bored. Bored and—though he hated to admit it—done. He'd set out to do what he planned with his hotel chains: bury himself in work to forget that his family was falling apart and to create the largest chain of hotels across the country. But what now?

Where did you go when you realized your entire life had been focused on work and business? What did he do now that it just wasn't enough? He'd even asked his friend.

Jack hadn't had any answers for him, other than to tell him he'd help find buyers if Gabe wanted out. Well, that and to encourage Gabe to find the right girl, settle down and have kids like Jack—but Gabe had a feeling that wasn't exactly in the cards for him.

Then again, a few years ago, who would have thought it would be for Jack?

"Hey, Jack," he said into the phone.

"You sound like shit, Gabe."

This brought a bark of laughter from Gabe. "Thanks, man. So nice of you not only to notice, but to point it out."

"More of the same?" Jack asked.

"Yeah." Gabe paused. "I think I'm done, Jack. I want out."

The line was quiet for a minute, and he could picture his friend leaning back in his chair, his expression inscrutable.

"Good. I think that's good," Jack said, surprising the hell out of Gabe.

"I thought you'd tell me to wait, not to sell. That my hotels are everything to me."

"Are they?" Jack asked.

Now it was Gabe's turn to be quiet.

"No. Not anymore," he finally said. "I thought for a while there I might start a new chain or something, but...."

He didn't finish. He didn't have to. He knew Jack understood.

"But you're finished," Jack said, reading Gabe's mind.

"Yeah. I am."

"All right. I've got a few groups that would be interested in buying you out. I don't think there's any single investor ready to take over your majority share, but I've got some ideas. Let me make some calls and I'll get back to you in a few days."

"Thanks, Jack. I appreciate it," Gabe said, refusing to question whether he was doing the right thing. He still had no idea what he'd do once the deal was done. He didn't actually *need* to work, but the idea of retiring and sitting on his ass at the age of thirty-nine didn't appeal either.

"And I have an idea for a new project for you," Jack said, his tone cryptic.

"Oh yeah, what's that?"

Jack Sutton was known for having the Midas touch, and he was also always trying something new and interesting—which was exactly what Gabe needed. Passing up anything Jack offered would be a mistake.

"I'll tell you about it the next time I see you. You coming home for Maddie's birthday party?" Jack asked.

"Of course," he said and a grin found its way to his face before he realized it. No matter what was going on in his life, the mention of Jack and Kelly's two-year-old daughter always brought a smile to his face. "I'll be in town sometime tomorrow morning. I'll see you guys Saturday."

"Great. I think she's expecting you to buy her a pony," Jack joked.

Gabe knew perfectly well Kelly would kill him if he spoiled Maddie *that* much. Besides, you didn't buy two-year-olds ponies, did you?

Gabe laughed and stepped out onto the terrace that over-looked New York City. The night air was warm, having only dropped a few degrees when the sun slipped out of sight beneath the horizon that evening. He leaned against the edge of the railing about to press Jack for more details about his mysterious project, when noise from below drew his attention.

"Hey, Jack, I gotta go—I'll see you Saturday," he said and disconnected.

Gabe looked down on the front entrance of the hotel. The paparazzi were hawking the door. It was expected tonight with PJ arriving, but he hadn't thought they'd see quite the number jock-eying for position on the sidewalk outside the hotel.

What the hell? Three more of the vulture-like paps had just walked up.

Gabe grabbed his iPhone and punched PJ's name into a search engine then scanned the top headlines.... He bit back a curse when the news flashed on the small screen and didn't have to watch much of the video to know why the scumbags waited at the hotel entrance to get at her tonight.

Kurt Tolleson was a dirtbag who cheated on PJ like the idiot that he was. Gabe couldn't imagine why a man would be willing to walk away from PJ Cantrell. An asshat like Kurt Tolleson had never deserved her in the first place.

When Gabe asked PJ about it shortly after the breakup appeared in the news, she'd been good and ticked off. *But this?*

Having the public see her humiliation.... She had to be reeling from this.

Movement on the street below pulled Gabe's attention back to the front entrance and he watched as PJ's car pulled up to the curb. The driver stayed in the car while one bodyguard stepped from the front of the car and opened the back door. *Where the hell was her other bodyguard?*

Gabe hoped to see him appear from the back, but no. Only PJ stepped out.

He couldn't make out her face, but he knew it was her. Her coppery red mane of hair and petite body would register with him anywhere. Register and make him hard as a rock in an instant, though he'd learned how to control that reaction around her. They were friends and nothing more.

Gabe growled and went back inside, picking up the hotel phone that sat on a side table near the balcony doors. Whenever he stayed in one of his suites, his line was directly routed to the general manager of that location or to the manager-on-duty when the GM was out. He didn't know who picked up and at the moment, he didn't care.

"Get more security out front. PJ just arrived and she only has one bodyguard with her. Get our guys out there now," he ordered before hanging up and going back outside.

He wanted to run down to her himself and stand between her and the world, but he wouldn't make it down there in time.

As he watched, someone with a camera reached right past the useless man in a suit trying to block access to PJ. The camera man yanked PJ around as he held his camera up in her face, snapping off shots the whole time. It took her bodyguard too damn long to get the guy off her.

Gabe watched as his staff poured out the front doors and surrounded PJ, whisking her into the lobby and away from the crowd.

In only minutes PJ would step into the elevator. He hoped she remembered his invitation and headed to his tower instead of going up to her suite.

Two years ago, he'd told her if she was looking for privacy or a friend to talk to, she could come up to his penthouse when he was at the hotel at the same time she was—which was often. Over time, they talked more and more frequently because they were both night owls.

He hoped on a night like this, when she had to be feeling angry and hurt by the betrayal of her privacy, she'd come to him.

Shoving his keycard in his back pocket, he drew a shirt over his head before stepping out to the private elevator entrance. He knew within minutes she was on her way up. Only he, his secretary, and PJ had the key fob that would allow them to enter the penthouse elevator.

Gabe paced until the elevator chimed her arrival, and smiled slightly when PJ's gaze fell on him immediately.

"Pru," he breathed out, using her first name rather than the initials the world used to address her. She always laughed at him for that, but he liked her full name. Prudence Jane. No one other than her family used it any longer. When she'd been 'discovered' she had been using the nickname PJ and that was part of her branding to the world.

She blinked those long, sexy eyelashes his way and he saw she was fighting back tears.

"You saw?" she asked. He didn't know if she was asking about the video or what had happened with the photographers down below, but he nodded.

"You holding up?" he asked, but he wanted to kick himself. He knew she'd say yes, even when it was clear she wasn't okay.

"I'm okay," she said but her teeth caught her bottom lip and he knew she was anything but okay.

He wanted to reach out and hold her, comfort her. But they'd never had that kind of relationship, though at times he felt so close to her it stunned him.

They had spent hours talking on the rooftops of his hotels, and it hadn't been that long ago that Gabe had started to feel a lot more than friendship toward her. But Pru, so much younger than him, had never indicated she wanted more from him.

For whatever reason, Gabe Sawyer—a man who routinely dated models and actresses and other people in the spotlight—froze up a little when he got around Pru Cantrell. He was sure he came across as some stiff CEO, and he didn't blame her for thinking that.

He was ten years older than her and was usually wearing a suit or a tux when he saw her. He glanced down at his jeans and bare feet and cringed. Well...until today.

"I just wasn't really up to going to bed," she said with a little laugh, and Gabe's mind immediately filled with images of her in his bed. He pushed them aside as he always did when he was with her.

"Come inside?" Gabe asked, gesturing over his shoulder to the stairs that led to his suite. He'd never invited her in before. Would she think he was trying to take advantage? Or would she understand he just wanted to be there for her after the night she'd had?

Gabe felt his heart kick as she nodded yes and followed him up the stairs.

PJ gulped and stared at Gabe's bare feet as he led her into his suite that was an exact duplicate of hers, but located on the opposite tower of the hotel. She was in *Gabe Sawyer's* hotel room. And, good lord, why couldn't she take her eyes off his feet? How were feet sexy?

They're not.

Except *those* particular bare feet topped by *those* soft, faded jeans were distinctly sexy. They were somehow hot as hell. But she'd always appreciated his good looks.

Everything about Gabe was hot as hell, from his deep-brown eyes to his almost-black hair that sometimes got a tiny bit messy late at night—when PJ itched to comb it back into place with her fingers.

Sometimes the attraction made it difficult for her to talk coherently and PJ just clammed up around him. She felt like a teenage idiot around Gabe, not a grown woman with a career that demanded she regularly make small talk with all kinds of people. Around Gabe, she just couldn't think of any intelligent thing to say.

Gabe didn't seem to have any issues around her. He tossed his keycard on the table by the entrance and nodded toward the couch in the living room.

"You hungry, Pru? I was planning to make an omelet. I do mine with egg whites, but I can add whole eggs to yours. Have a seat and I'll whip up something for us."

He didn't seem to care that it was two in the morning, and he sure didn't seem to be obsessing over her presence in his suite the way she was.

"Um, thanks." She lowered herself to the couch, but then quickly got up and followed him into the kitchen, going on tip-toes to look over his shoulder as he leaned into the fridge. "You cook?"

Gabe stood, pulling a carton of eggs and an armload of veggies out of the fridge. When he spun around to answer her question, it put them almost toe to toe. PJ's breath caught.

His gaze met hers with an intensity that made her mouth drop open in an involuntary plea for him to kiss her. *OMG.* PJ blinked and stepped back, realizing she'd put herself much too close to him. Much closer than he probably intended.

He'd always treated her like a friend, a kid sister even.

Nothing more. With most men, that's what she wanted —friendship.

With Gabe? Well, she'd known for a few years that she wanted a lot more than friendship from Gabe.

What am I thinking? Someone has my journal, and all of my secrets could be shared with the world at any moment...and I'm lusting after a man who's utterly unreachable.

Gabe cleared his throat and dumped the ingredients on the counter.

"Yeah. I got tired of having room service about...." He raised his eyes to the ceiling as if calculating something in his head. "Oh, eight years ago."

The grin he threw her way made her panties melt. PJ slipped onto one of the bar stools that lined the counter separating the kitchen from the spacious living room. Still, he continued to affect her, and she pressed her legs together to douse some of the heat she felt.

"*Mmm.* I tried cooking for a while for that same reason," she said. "It g-got...complicated," she stuttered. *What an idiot.*

Gabe raised his eyebrows at her as he whisked the eggs together and then tossed the vegetables to sauté in a pan on the burner.

PJ felt her cheeks burn as she tried to figure out how to explain herself without sounding like an arrogant, spoiled celebrity. Gabe helped her out.

"Oh, right, shopping. I guess going to the grocery store can be a bit tough."

She nodded and shrugged. "My mom and I used to cook together when I was a kid. I loved it. When she was with me on tour, in the early days, she would shop and we could still cook together. But now she doesn't go on tour with me very often. I tried having Ellis get stuff for me, but it's weird having someone else do your shopping. You know? And grocery shopping online isn't really the same."

Gabe nodded and turned his attention back to the stove. The smell of the melted butter and onions made her stomach growl, and she realized he really knew his way around a kitchen. Her suspicions were confirmed when Gabe placed a plate in front of her a few minutes later and she took her first bite.

She may have groaned in appreciation a little more loudly than she intended, but the omelet melted on her tongue and the sound just slipped out before she could censor herself.

Gabe stilled, his laser eyes on hers, but then quickly moved back to plating his own omelet.

"Good?" he asked, grinning again. "When did your parents leave the tour?"

"They came on tour after I left rehab and stayed until I was nineteen. By then, I had a good manager and support staff around me so they were able to go back to their lives. They come out for a week or two with me each year now, but they haven't been with me steadily for a long time."

PJ looked at Gabe's intense gaze and wondered if it was inappropriate to fantasize about pulling him across the counter and stripping his shirt off to reveal his chiseled chest.... Would it be wrong to ask to have him for dessert?

So wrong, PJ. So very wrong.

She blushed and focused on her plate before she made a fool of herself. The last thing she needed to think about was sex. She had a lot bigger problems on her plate than a delicious omelet, and the simple fact that her sex life with Kurt would be plastered all over the Internet by now.

Though, for the moment, that seemed a world away; she needed to figure out who had her journal before they sold more of it. Her thoughts must have shown on her face.

"Hey," Gabe said, his voice soft, "you thinking about that jerk again?"

PJ cleared her throat and shrugged her shoulders.

She couldn't tell him the other part of the story, the part

where her whole world could be torn down around her. The part where her family would be destroyed—they'd be more affected than she would by what might come out in the press 'reveal.'

PJ pulled her phone from her pocket when the vibrating she'd been ignoring got to be too much. Her mom.

Are you okay?

Not even remotely, PJ thought, but she didn't tell her mother that.

Yeah. Hanging out with a friend. Talk to you in the morning.

The next text was from Debra, her manager: *Got a response out to the media. Do you want to do interviews?*

No, PJ answered. She had almost a week off before her next show, and she'd decided to take it off and bury her head in the sand for a bit. *I'd rather ignore Kurt and the media for now.*

You got it, came Debra's response a minute later. Debra was a lot less intense than Lydia but just as good at her job. She knew how to manage PJ's career without managing PJ as if she was a product instead of a person.

It was why Lydia was only her tour manager. She wouldn't be able to handle Lydia managing her world on the global basis Debra did.

A few seconds passed, and PJ knew Gabe was watching her as he ate his omelet. She tucked her phone back in her pocket and finished the last bite of her meal.

"So what else do you cook? Breakfast food only, or are you more versatile than that?" she asked and was relieved when Gabe seemed happy to go with the light conversation.

"I'm not all that bad with comfort foods—pot roast, meatloaf. I make a mean chicken pot pie," he said with that grin that made her legs quake.

PJ wondered if maybe she was in some sort of denial. Rather than dealing with the fact someone out there had her very personal and private journal, and she could only assume would be revealing its contents to the highest bidder as soon as they could get a buyer, she was here lusting after a man who probably still thought of her as the nineteen-year-old she was when they met.

She'd been nineteen and he'd been twenty-nine. And of course, he'd seen her as a kid. He was always kind to her, respectful, making sure his hotels provided the highest level of care for her whenever she stayed in any of them.

That was one of the reasons she always inserted a clause in her contract that provided she be put up in a Grand Tower if there was one within twenty miles of her concert site. He'd always treated her the same, and she assumed he still saw her as that nineteen-year-old girl.

And then, a few years ago, they started talking more, spending time together at his hotels, outside of events and fundraisers. She'd discovered she liked talking to him, and he seemed to understand her, to understand her need to have someone to simply listen without making a big deal out of who she was.

She started to see him as more than just a friend, but he'd never given any indication he saw her in any kind of romantic way. Knowing her luck, he saw her as a little sister; someone to be taken care of—not someone to sweep off her feet with a soul-wrenchingly hot kiss that would melt them both to the core like she sometimes imagined.

Not where your imagination should be headed, PJ.

"Hmm. You go from egg white and veggie omelets to heavy, rich comfort foods. What's up with that?" She scrunched her nose at him and he laughed.

"I try to eat pretty healthy most of the time, but who doesn't need some good comfort food once in a while? Most of the time I make stir fries or baked chicken and vegetables, but some days are mac and cheese days, right?"

PJ nodded, not able to lose the smile on her face. She really did know all about those mac and cheese days.

This felt good, just hanging out with someone who seemed to have no expectations. No agenda.

He was certainly used to being around people like her in his line of work. And, he had no reason to want something from her. He had his own money, his own fame—and he already knew she loved his hotels.

There wasn't anything she could give him besides what he seemed to be asking for: her friendship. Even though, at times, she wanted more from him than that, there was something liberating about knowing he wasn't trying to get something more or to use her for his own gain. She could be herself with him in a way she couldn't with anyone else.

"Ice cream's my weakness," she said. "My team keeps the freezer stocked with these salted-caramel ice cream bars. They're covered in chocolate with chunks of pretzels in them. They're amazing." PJ was a little mortified to realize she moaned again while talking about her ice cream bars.

She let her eyes glance up to Gabe's and caught the heated intensity of his look.

Then, with the blink of an eye it was washed away.

What was that about?

"Tell me," he said as he picked up his now-empty plate and grabbed hers before heading to the sink. "Do you think it was Kurt who stole your journal and leaked it to the press? More publicity for him? When did you have it last?"

PJ's stomach dropped. She'd forgotten about her journal for one blissful minute.

"No. Well, maybe. I don't really know." She felt even more stupid, not knowing how someone got her journal or who might have it.

Would she put it past Kurt to do something like that? No, not at all. Erika was no fan of PJ's either. Despite the fact Kurt had dumped PJ for her, Erika had harassed PJ for weeks afterward, texting that PJ better stay away from her man and all that.

PJ didn't need that kind of drama in her world. Lord knew her life on the road gave her enough drama as it was. She'd changed her number and tried to forget about Kurt and Erika.

"Where did you keep it?" Gabe asked the question gently, as though he wanted to be sure she knew he was only asking the question to be supportive.

PJ shook her head and felt the telltale prick of tears behind her eyes. "That's the thing. *Nobody* knew I kept a journal. And, I mean nobody. I never wrote in it in front of other people. Only when I was by myself at night. I kept it on a USB drive that I hid in a tear in the lining of my purse. The drive even looked like an old lipstick so anyone who found it would think it was makeup."

"It's not on a cloud or backed up on your computer or anything?" he asked.

"No. I should have just deleted it after each entry, you know? I mean really, what's the point of saving all that?" She shrugged. "I just got in the habit of it in rehab and never stopped."

He raised an eyebrow at her. "That's a lot of years. You were what, sixteen when you went to rehab?"

"Fifteen. I wanted to get that whole addiction thing out of the way early in life. Call me an overachiever." The comment got the laugh she was looking for.

Gabe grabbed two bottles of water and tugged her toward the couch, settling down on one end while she sank into the other.

"Someone knew it was there," Gabe said returning the conversation to her journal.

PJ bit her lip and nodded. "Whoever took it had to be really close to me. I keep my purse with me all the time. If I don't have it, Lydia or Ellis carries it."

She shook her head. "Maybe one of them left it where a fan or stagehand could access it backstage—but I doubt it. They're as protective of my privacy as I am. They didn't know they were protecting my journal, but they know my cell phone is in there and fans can go crazy trying to grab a piece of me. They wouldn't have left that lying around for anyone to pick up."

Whoever did this was someone she trusted or someone her family or team had trusted. And that made all of this that much harder to handle.

CHAPTER 3

Gabe couldn't believe they'd been up all night talking together. When PJ had looked so sad talking about her missing journal, he changed the topic to something lighter.

They'd spent the last five hours talking about books, music, movies, pets they'd had when they were young—pets they wished they could have now but didn't have the time for—and food. They talked a lot about food. PJ's eyes lit up, and she became animated when she talked about the things she loved.

She told him about her writing process and how song ideas seemed to build in her mind, until it felt like she'd explode and she had to write them down. If he tried to explain that to someone, it would sound stupid. Coming from her, it somehow seemed magical and otherworldly.

Wow, you're a sap.

He was, though. He was a total and complete sap where Pru Cantrell was concerned. She smiled weakly at him now, the exhaustion clear in her face. It wasn't just that she was tired from staying up all night talking.

It was a real, bone-deep exhaustion from the weight and the pressure on her. He could see it. Her life was filled with pressure on a good day, given her tour schedule and the demands of recording new material. Add to it the additional stress of the missing journal, and it was obvious she was at a breaking point.

"I should probably head back to my room," she said, looking at the door...but her voice told him she didn't want to.

"You don't have a show for another six days," he said, and then wanted to kick himself when she looked at him sharply, no doubt surprised he knew her schedule.

"True," she said slowly, drawing the syllable out.

"Do you have interviews or appearances lined up?" he asked.

"No," she said with a bit of a laugh. "This was supposed to be six days of rest and relaxation. I haven't taken that much time off in a long time. Now it'll be six days of hiding out and trying to ignore phone calls, and the constant temptation to jump on the Internet to see what's happening."

"You should come to Connecticut with me." *What? Where did that come from?*

"Connecticut?"

Hell. Why not?

"I keep a house there that no one knows about. I bought it a few years ago so I'd have a place to go where I'm not offered room service and turndown at night. No one knows about it except my friends. We can take my private jet. You can just fall off the grid for a few days, get some real rest."

He could see her thinking about it, chewing on her bottom lip as she eyed him through lowered lashes. He didn't want to pressure her, but man, he suddenly wanted to be the one to be able to take her away from this shit situation she was in. The one to give her the respite she needed while the whirlwind of her life settled down for a bit.

And, he wouldn't lie to himself. He'd had a better time with her tonight than he had with any of the women he'd dated. Just talking to her, with nothing sexual between them other than the way his imagination ran away every time she moaned over a bite of food or laughed at one of his jokes, was better than a lot of the nights he'd spent wrapped in some naked woman's arms and legs.

He'd been resisting the sexual attraction and wouldn't act on it when she was so vulnerable, but at least he could be there for her. He could support her and help her through this without acting on the chemistry that shot between them whenever they were together.

"No strings attached, PJ. I promise. I'm headed there anyway to see some friends and go to a two-year-old's birthday party. What could be better than balloons and cake? Just two friends, getting away for a while. That's all it will be."

It's not all I want it to be, but I'll take it.

PJ had never shown any inclination to hit on him—which made sense. The first time they'd met, she'd only been eighteen or nineteen and he'd been twenty-nine. With her current age of twenty-nine and him at thirty-nine, it would be considered acceptable if something did happen between them, but he had a feeling she still saw him the same way she always had. Old.

PJ looked as though she struggled to come to a decision. She finally nodded her head, slowly. "All right. If you're going anyway, I'd love to tag along."

CHAPTER 4

*P*J knew she needed to face her team and call her parents before heading to Connecticut. Her phone was filled with missed calls and unanswered texts.

She didn't blame them for being concerned, and she knew they'd need to hear from her before she left—to confirm she wasn't drunk. It might have been thirteen years since her addiction had almost ruined her career, but she knew it was hard for her parents to forget their struggle to save her. To straighten her out.

And at a time like this, it would be easy for them to think she would turn back to drinking to numb the emotions clobbering her.

PJ made her way across the hotel to her suite in the opposite tower and shut the door behind her, relieved neither Lydia nor Ellis waited there for her.

She dialed her mother's number and wasn't surprised that she answered on only the second ring. She checked her watch. Her parents wouldn't leave for their small bookstore outside Deep Creek Lake in Maryland for at least another hour.

They'd gone through so much with her early on in her career with the addiction and pregnancy. It always made her feel good to picture them in their bookstore doing what they loved—happy and relaxed again instead of on edge and worried for her. That would all change if her journal was released to the media. Her fault again.

"Hey, Mom." PJ could hear her father in the background.

"Hi, sweetheart. Your father wants to know how you're doing. Did you book extra interviews for this week to respond to Kurt's comments?" her mother asked, drawing a wince from PJ.

It was hard to talk about Kurt's review of her performance in bed with her parents. *Ugh.*

Her mother didn't wait for her response before continuing. "You don't have to respond to that...that...." PJ almost laughed as her mother sought the right word to describe Kurt. Her mother didn't swear. Ever. But, it sounded like she was dying to right now.

"*Ninny,*" her mother finally finished. PJ laughed at her mother's choice of words. Yup. *Ninny* was about as nasty as her mom was going to get.

"Debra called earlier to fill us in," her mother said. "She put out a short press release so you can leave it at that, PJ. Don't feel like you have to engage him or the press over this. Personally, I think we should ignore it. We don't need to give him any more attention than he's already gotten."

"Yeah, I'm going to ignore it and let the whole thing die down, Mom," PJ finally answered when her mom took a breath during her diatribe.

PJ knew this wasn't going to just die down on its own. She opened her mouth to tell her mom what was coming, but she didn't know how to say the words.

She chickened out. "I'm going to take a few days off. I'll meet the team in Denver for the next show, but I just need to take a break for a bit."

"Where're you headed to? Do you want to come here?" her mom asked.

PJ blushed, thankful her parents couldn't see her through the phone. "I'm going to Connecticut to spend a few days with Gabe Sawyer and his friends. He's headed there and offered to let me come, just to get away from everything."

She tried to play it off as if it wasn't a big deal, but really the idea of spending a week with Gabe, even as friends, made her stomach do backflips.

PJ could almost envision her father's eyebrows going up and wasn't surprised to hear his voice coming through the phone, although it was muffled, as if he were speaking over her mother's shoulder.

"Gabe Sawyer, as in owner of The Grand Tower...that Gabe Sawyer?"

"Do you really think that's wise, Prudence?" her mother asked.

"*Mmm hmm,*" she murmured. She should have known she wouldn't slip that by them so easily.

"Pru, don't you think he's, well.... He seems to love the limelight a bit much, don't you think? Is it really wise to be seen with him right now? What if he's just hoping to capitalize on your spotlight?" Her father must have taken the phone from her mother. His voice was coming through more clearly now.

PJ shook her head. "No, Dad. Gabe doesn't like all the attention any more than I do most of the time. In fact, he's managed to keep his house in Connecticut completely off the radar so far. Only his friends know he has it, so the chances of us being found there are slim to none."

As she spoke, she tossed a few outfits into a backpack. She'd ask Ellis to swing by and have her other luggage taken to the tour bus so it would make it out to Denver and be there when she arrived to perform.

"You're not... Well, w-what I mean is...are you two...?" Her mother, now seemingly back in control of the phone, all but stammered.

PJ rolled her eyes. "Oh for heaven's sake, you guys. I'm not a gullible teenager anymore. Gabe isn't looking for anything like that from me."

She might not be a teenager, but she couldn't bring herself to say the words sex and Gabe in the same sentence to her parents. This whole conversation was a lot more than she wanted to deal with right now, but she knew they had their reasons for worrying.

"Gabe is a friend. Nothing more. He has his own money, his own fame, and his pick of any woman he wants on the planet. Believe me, there's literally *nothing* Gabe could want from me."

PJ had to admit, saying that out loud hurt more than a bit. She'd had a crush on Gabe Sawyer for a long time. But the truth was, he only saw her as a friend—and that was all right. She was glad to have his friendship. It was all she could offer right now with the shape her world was in anyway. It was really all she needed.... Really.

Maybe if she kept telling herself that, she'd stop hoping for something more from him.

CHAPTER 5

*P*J gasped as she took in the large home at the crest of the circular drive. "It's incredible, Gabe."

The two-story, light-gray house with black shutters had a small carriage house off to the side of the driveway, and an enormous landscaped yard behind tall stone walls. There wouldn't be any issues about privacy here.

At least, not until the paparazzi got wind of her location and tried to climb the walls. At eight feet, they looked fairly formidable, but you never knew what people would try once the rest of the news in her personal journal broke.

PJ faltered a bit as her thoughts turned back to her journal, but she was determined to step away from all that for a while. She just wanted one week to rest before she had to face the storm that would surely hit soon.

When it did hit, she'd leave so she didn't destroy the oasis Gabe had here.

He pulled Pru's bag from the trunk of his car and took her arm to walk her up the steps. The contact sent a zing through her and she didn't try to fight the attraction. She just had to keep it from showing, that's all.

"Wait till you see the back. I bought it for the privacy, but the view of Long Island Sound can't be beat, and the outdoor patio is amazing. I had the caretakers stock the kitchen for us, so other than going over to Jack's house, we can hide out here."

He pulled her through the foyer and down a long hallway that led straight out the back of the house. They ignored the formal dining room, sitting room, and living room and landed in a large, open kitchen. From there, French doors spilled out onto the stone patio in the back yard.

"Oh my gosh," PJ said, knowing she sounded like an idiot, as she looked out onto the sparkling water of the infinity swimming pool that appeared to fall off into the ocean in an incredible optical illusion. An immaculately manicured lawn sloped to the ocean, and there were tennis courts off to the side of the patio.

Gabe nudged her shoulder and pointed to their left where a full outdoor kitchen and grill sat next to a large stone fireplace.

"Ohhhhhh. It's a completely perfect oasis," PJ said, and she moaned again as she looked at the teak chairs in front of the outdoor stone fireplace with the Jacuzzi tub nearby.

PJ wondered how far they'd have to go to get to the party at Jack's house the following day. She honestly wasn't sure she wanted to leave the sanctuary Gabe had just shown her.

"Where does Jack live?"

Gabe's face broke into a wide grin—one of his grins that always made her breath catch, and her panties want to fly off and scream 'take me!'—if panties could scream.

"That's the best part." Gabe slipped his hand into hers and pulled her further out to the edge of the patio, then leaned a bit further and pointed to the right. The large stone wall continued around the side of the house, even blocking access to the ocean. PJ had seen a gate at the back of the yard and assumed that led to a private beach. But, now she saw another small gate in the wall and the roof of a large house beyond it.

"That's Jack's house," Gabe said.

PJ laughed. "You bought a house right next to your friend?"

Gabe nodded, and his grin widened if that was even possible. "I couldn't resist. That way, I know there won't be a psycho over there. And the guy on the other side of me is Andrew, Jack's best friend. He and his wife, Jill, will be at the party tomorrow. We all have the codes to each other's gates so we can cut through our yards. It's perfect. Chad lives about three houses up, so he and Jennie need to walk down the road or take the beach," he said, as if that were the greatest hardship in the world.

PJ just continued to shake her head, but she was smiling. She couldn't believe all his good friends owned houses so close to one another. What would she give to have that kind of life? Those kind of friends?

Anything, she realized. She had huge bank accounts and had invested in several profitable businesses, but now she saw the limitations of that. Building money wasn't much of a life.

She could see why Gabe was thinking of giving up his hotels. Everything he needed was right here. She would want to stay here full time, too, if she were him.

PJ's phone beeped in her purse.

"I should let you get settled in, I guess," he said, nodding in the direction of her bag.

PJ nodded. It felt a little awkward suddenly, now that they were really here, alone in his house together. "Yeah, I should check messages and touch base with Debra. Make sure everything's still on track for next week's shows. I'm sure Lydia's giving her hell. She's probably furious that I'm not adding interviews to the schedule this week. If Lydia had her way, she would have milked this episode for all the publicity she could get."

He ran his hand across her lower back as he guided her toward the house. "Let's get you to your room, then. I can start dinner while you take care of things."

Gabe showed her to a room just off the patio where they stood just moments earlier. The queen-sized bed was piled high with welcoming pillows and a vase of fresh flowers brightened the room, but it was the doorway leading out to a private side patio that drew her attention.

The French doors had an archway over them, and they practically beckoned her to go outside and sit in the sun. Teak furniture that matched the set on the patio created the perfect private sitting area. As with all of Gabe's hotels, everything she could want was set out for her—every luxury available to her.

"This is perfect, Gabe. Thank you," she said as he set her bag down on the bed.

"Let me know if you need anything. Something light for dinner?"

PJ wrinkled up her nose, drawing a laugh from Gabe.

"Comfort food, it is," he said, walking toward the bedroom door. "Double bacon, blue-cheese burgers and mashed potatoes coming right up. I'll throw a salad together on the side to fight off some of the guilt."

PJ laughed and then pulled her phone from her bag and sank down into an overstuffed wing chair in the corner of the room.

The laugh dried to dust in her throat as she read the line of text messages on her phone. She scrolled to see the phone number for the incoming texts, but the originating numbers were blocked.

How is that possible? Her phone number was kept under lock and key. Her parents, Debra, Lydia, Ellis, the band and a few friends had it. She was fairly sure Lydia and Ellis's mom had it since both her children worked so closely with PJ and she was friends with PJ's mom, but no one on that list would give it out. *Would they?*

PJ scrolled to the top text and read through to the bottom. They'd all come within minutes of one another and they read like the kind of sing-song teasing you might hear on a playground:

Did you think I was going to let you off the hook so easily, Pretty Prudence Cantrell?

Last night was just a taste of the hell you'll be going through in the weeks to come.

Did you cry yourself to sleep last night?

How many times do you think your baby cried himself to sleep without you?

Time to pay the price for your selfishness, Pretty Pru.

That answered the question of whether the person knew all her secrets. PJ closed her eyes and squeezed them until the tears she'd felt threatening backed off just a bit. Crying wouldn't change anything.

Her hands shook as she typed in a response.

What do you want?

She jumped when the phone beeped almost immediately.

Tsk tsk, Pretty Pru. I already told you that. You'll pay. It's that simple. The world has only seen what you've let them see. You have them all fooled. But not me. I know the truth. I know all your dirty little secrets. And, I plan to make your payment long and hard.

I can pay you for the journal. I'll pay you more than the newspapers will, she offered knowing that would mean spending most of her fortune, but she didn't care.

So like a spoiled rich brat to think she can buy her way out of everything. I can't be bought.

PJ took a deep breath and pulled up her contacts, then pushed the entry for her uncle and aunt, Brian and Susie Chambers. She listened to the ringing on the other end of the phone as her mind raced through the list of people who could be behind this.

"Hello." It was Brian who picked up the phone.

"It's me," PJ said and realized she sounded awful. The words came out sounding more like a sob than anything intelligible.

"Pru, how're you holding up?" Brian asked, and she could hear the genuine concern in his voice. It took several minutes for her to get it together enough to answer him.

"Uh, it's not good, Brian."

"I know, hon. Susie saw it on one of the talk shows this morning. Your mom said you were handling things okay. That you're taking a few days off?"

PJ shook her head even though he couldn't see her over the phone. "I didn't tell Mom and Dad all of it."

There was a slight pause on the other end before her uncle answered. "Didn't tell them what, Pru?"

"Whoever leaked those things from my journal—they have the whole thing. They have all of it, from the time I left rehab on. They know, Brian."

PJ could hear him talking in the background before Susie's voice came on the phone.

"Are you sure they have it all? Maybe they just got pieces of it?" Susie asked, and PJ lost her fight against the tears as she answered.

"The journal is missing—they have it. And they texted me. They know about the baby." PJ's shoulders slumped, and she pulled her knees up to her chest as she waited for a response.

"Did they ask for money?" Susie asked.

"I tried to buy it back but they don't want that. They want me to pay for my selfishness. I don't know who it could be." She could hear more muffled talk as Brian and Susie spoke.

Brian came back on the phone. "Susie and I need to talk about this, Pru, but we'll call you soon. I want you to tell your parents about this, you hear me? You need to let them know what's going on so they can increase your security and help you deal with this if it does come out."

"I'll tell them soon, Brian. I just want a few days, and I'm in a safe location right now. No one knows where I am."

And, no one was supposed to have your cell phone number, either.

It was stupid really, but PJ was twenty-nine years old. She didn't want to run to her parents to fix her problems anymore. Lord knew, they'd had to do enough for her when she was younger. They shouldn't have to carry her through this now. Whatever this person wanted, she'd handle it herself.

~

Gabe looked up and studied her face when PJ entered the kitchen. She looked a bit like she might have been crying, but he didn't want to push her with questions.

He couldn't imagine having his private thoughts spread out on the Internet for everyone to see. That had to hurt, even though she'd put up a pretty good front so far.

"Dinner's almost ready," he said, tossing the freshly sliced tomatoes onto the top of the salad. "I thought we'd eat out on the patio?"

PJ nodded at him but didn't speak, and that's when Gabe was sure—she had been crying. He came around the kitchen island and pulled her into him, tucking her head under his chin and rubbing her back.

The gesture had been meant to comfort her but she felt so effing good in his arms—so perfectly right when he held her close. He could feel her small arms come around his back to hold him, and he really didn't want to let her go.

The disappointment he felt when she pulled away was tempered only slightly by the smile on her face when he looked down at her.

"Thanks. I needed that," she said.

"Anytime," he said. *Any and every time you want.*

Gabe crossed to the island and grabbed the salad and plates. "The burgers should be ready out on the grill and everything else is already out there."

"It smells amazing," she said as they walked to the patio together.

Gabe set the salad down and went about plating the burgers

and scooping heaps of mashed potatoes onto the plate. He looked down at the heaping plate then up at PJ's tiny frame.

"Oh, you probably can't eat all this, can you?" he asked and turned to scoop some of the potatoes back. He'd served her the kind of portion he might hand to Jack or Andrew for a first round.

PJ stabbed at his hand with a fork. "Back off my potatoes, mister," she said and pulled the plate from his hands. "Mine," she said, twisting to guard the food with her body as she eyed him suspiciously. Damn she was funny; he couldn't help but laugh.

"Something to drink?" Gabe's face heated. With her history of alcohol addiction, he shouldn't offer her anything alcoholic, he thought quickly. Why hadn't he considered that earlier?

He had no idea how his caretakers had stocked the fridge, and he hadn't thought to ask for nonalcoholic drinks. "Water? Coke? Um——" He looked toward the small fridge in the outdoor kitchen, not sure what was there.

"Water's great," PJ said as she sat in one of the chairs. If she noticed his discomfort about what to offer her, she didn't let it show.

Gabe grabbed two bottles of water and shut the fridge with his foot then retrieved his plate from next to the grill. A flick of a light switch with his elbow had flames dancing to life in the gas firepit as he lowered himself into the chair next to PJ's.

PJ moaned when she took a bite of the bacon, blue cheese concoction he'd cooked up for them and Gabe felt his whole body still. If she didn't knock off that adorable habit she had of moaning when something good crossed those lips, he wouldn't make it through the week without a lot of cold showers and hand lotion.

"It's okay if you want to drink," she said in between bites, and Gabe's first thoughts jumped to whiskey.

Shots of whiskey might help him get through this alive and moderately sane without too many fantasies about other ways he could make her moan, or what she might sound like when he took her soft nipple into his mouth and made it peak under his tongue.

He shook his head instead, half in answer to her and half in an attempt to banish thoughts of PJ's breasts from his mind. "I'm good with water. Burger okay?" he asked.

"More than okay. It's amazing. Maybe that's what you should do now. Become a chef. Or open a chain of restaurants. World-class restaurants with nothing but comfort food."

Gabe laughed as PJ took another big bite and then followed that with a forkful of mashed potatoes.

And, another moan. Dear Lord, woman. Gabe wanted to lean across his chair and swallow those moans of hers in a kiss. But, that was the last thing she needed and he wouldn't do that to her now. He'd be what she needed: a friend.

He shifted his plate in his lap. It wouldn't look great for her to see exactly how much she affected him. She'd probably run and hide if she knew the kind of thoughts he had about her.

"No?" she asked, seemingly unaware of the effect she had on him. "Don't like the restaurant idea? *Hmmm.* A cooking show! I bet all the housewives would watch you cook. You know, jeans and an apron? Nothing much else?" PJ said with a mischievous grin. "I bet if you demonstrated how to make a bowl of cereal with no shirt on it would be a hit."

Gabe turned to look at her as she laughed next to him. Her whole face lit up when she laughed, and desire flew through him hard and fast and demanding.

To hell with it.

He leaned across the space between the two Adirondack chairs and swept her mouth with his, quickly. Just a taste. Just the taste he'd been dreaming about for years. He pulled back and looked into her stunned eyes.

Shit.

"I'm sorry," he said, but didn't move away as his eyes locked with hers. "I just wanted to see what that felt like. What you taste like."

PJ's eyes were big and round and Gabe cursed again in his head. He really shouldn't have done that. This wasn't what she needed right now. He knew that. Hell, he'd been telling himself that for days whenever he tried to curb his desire.

Then she leaned in, and one of her hands snaked behind his head and pulled him to her—back to her mouth—and he was lost.

Utterly lost in the feel of her lips as they connected with his, the feel of her tongue as it tangled with his own, the feel of her body when he slid his arms around her and pulled her closer to him.

Gabe allowed himself to get lost in her for just a moment, before pulling away and taking a breath.

"Shit," he said, not meeting her eyes.

PJ was still and quiet next to him, and he could hear her trying to settle her breathing. It was likely as much of a challenge for her as it had been for him. That was one hell of a kiss.

"Well," PJ said with a little laugh. "That's what you want to hear after you kiss a man. 'Shit.'"

Gabe's eyes flew to hers and he ran a hand through his hair. "I'm sorry, PJ. I really didn't mean to do that. I didn't bring you here for that. I didn't come here planning to take advantage of you like some...some... Shit." Gabe didn't know what else to say.

He watched PJ's face, trying to get a read on her thoughts, but she remained silent.

"This is probably the last thing you need right now, Pru." Something flickered behind her eyes and she sat up straight.

"You know what? You're right." She nodded and gave him a tentative smile before setting her half-eaten meal next to his and pushing to her feet. The distraction might be nice, but getting involved right now wasn't a good idea, no matter how strong the attraction between them ran. "I should get some sleep, I think. I'm pretty beat."

Gabe stood and nodded as she walked into the house, and he watched her turn toward her room.

What the hell had he been thinking? They were barely a few hours into their trip and he had been all over her. Why on earth had he thought he could bring her here and keep his hands off her?

Gabe tossed the leftover food in the trash and left the dishes in the sink. He'd deal with them in the morning. For now, he wanted to grab his swim trunks and hit the ocean. Maybe the cold water would knock some sense into him and cool his desire.

CHAPTER 6

*P*J took longer than she normally would have to get ready the following morning. She knew damned well it was because she didn't want to face Gabe after that kiss.

She was embarrassed, but more so, she was afraid things would be awkward and uneasy between her and Gabe now. The relationship she'd built with him in the last few years was surprisingly important to her.

A huff of laughter escaped her as she thought about how absurd it was that she could label the friendship she'd developed with the man who owned her favorite hotels as one of her best friendships. Yeah, just showed you how ridiculous her life had become.

She glanced at her guitar sitting in the corner of the room and promised herself she'd take it out to the back patio and play later today.

Putting her phone into the bedside drawer so she could ignore the dumpster fire her world had become, she took a deep breath and opened the door. Time to face Gabe.

When she walked in the kitchen, she found him sitting on a bar stool at the counter, drinking coffee and reading the paper.

Her heart kicked into overdrive when he looked up at her and went to the restaurant style espresso machine that took up a large portion of his counter.

"Latte?"

When he turned to look at her, PJ's cheeks flushed with heat under his gaze. All he'd done was offer her coffee, but all she could think about was the kiss. And how he'd stopped it.

"Thanks," she said, trying to force her thoughts in another direction.

"I have an idea for today," Gabe said, seemingly happy to ignore the humiliating tension between them as he steamed milk.

PJ looked up. "Hopefully nothing that involves going out in public?"

Gabe grinned and shook his head, setting aside the newspaper he'd been reading.

"I thought I'd make four different kinds of popcorn—"

PJ held up a hand. "Four different kinds?"

"Cheese, butter and sea salt, ranch, and butter and brown sugar."

"Yes."

Gabe laughed. "You haven't heard the rest of my plan."

"You had me at butter and brown sugar." She tilted her head. "And at cheese, butter and sea salt, and ranch."

"Done," he said. "You take your coffee to the couch and I'll start on the popcorn buffet. Do you want anything else for breakfast? Eggs? Fruit?"

PJ frowned. "You don't need to wait on me, Gabe. I can make a piece of toast or something."

He waved her off and shooed her toward the couch. "I like cooking. I'll make us something for breakfast and get the popcorn ready. You're in charge of pulling up Harry Potter and the Sorcerer's Stone on TV."

She couldn't help but laugh at that. "Are we marathoning them all?"

"Hell, yes. That's the plan. We spend the day on the couch

with blankets and snacks and watch Harry defeat Voldemort. It's therapeutic."

"I see. Does this come from some kind of expert or did you come up with this yourself?"

The grin he gave her was one of those panty-melting variety and she was pretty sure he didn't even know he did it. Being sexy was just his default.

"This was all me. But trust me, I know how to do a lazy day ignoring the world right. I think I even have some Kit-Kats and Twix bars in the freezer. We can pull those out when we hit the third or fourth movie."

PJ shook her head but she went into the living room and flipped on the TV. Who was she to argue with that type of genius? Besides, curling up on the couch did sound like a great idea, and she hadn't honestly seen all of the movies. She'd missed the last three.

She listened as Gabe worked in the kitchen, hearing the crack of eggs. Was it wrong that she was hoping he was making her an omelet again? Probably.

But damn, that man could cook.

And kiss....

She shook off the memory of that kiss even as it made her squirm, doing things to her body that she didn't need just then.

She grabbed one of the throws he had folded on the couch and snuggled under it, flicking to the search function and finding the first Harry Potter movie.

She had it set up and ready to go when Gabe came in carrying a large tray with the omelets she'd been craving and fresh fruit. He hadn't been kidding about all the types of popcorn.

He settled on the other side of the couch and handed PJ her plate with fruit and eggs.

She was going to be addicted to the man's cooking by the end of the week.

As they watched Harry wake up in the cupboard under the

stairs, PJ whispered, "Can I ask you a serious question before we get too far into the movie?"

Gabe turned to her immediately, his entire focus on her. "Always."

PJ swallowed at the intensity of his attention but asked her question. "Can you make quiche?"

The way his smile spread slow and easy on his face and his eyes lit with amusement made her instantly relax.

"Damn straight I can make quiche." He lifted her feet and placed them in his lap tucking her cover around them before winking at her. "Tomorrow."

PJ felt her chest ease and she snuggled down to watch the movie, feeling lighter than she had in days. She lost herself in the comfort of sitting with Gabe and the unbeatable escapism of watching Harry discover a world filled with hidden doorways, chocolate frogs, banking goblins, and new best friends.

CHAPTER 7

hey watched fourteen of the twenty hours of Potter movies before calling it quits. A steady diet of popcorn, chips and salsa, and Reese's Pieces had PJ almost wishing they'd stuck to the fruit from breakfast. Almost.

She made a lame attempt at playing her guitar when they finally turned off the T.V. but it hadn't gone very far. The music that normally flowed through her seemed to have dried up with the stress of the last couple of days.

She was now walking on the beach, a light sweater wrapped around her shoulders. Gabe had assured her she wouldn't run into any large crowds on the private beach and he was right. With her hair tucked under a floppy sunhat and sun glasses shading her eyes, she was pretty well disguised.

The sand squished between her toes and the muscles in her legs seemed to thank her for the stretch after so many hours on the couch. She kept her head down, watching for the tiny shells that dotted the sand, usually showing up where the water seemed to have brushed them all together to form a line.

A bit of porcelain caught her eye and she picked it up, rubbing her hand over the soft surface. Battered by the sea, it had only come out more beautiful, smoothed of any sharp edge that it had once held, and PJ couldn't help but wonder if she would come out of this in the same way.

Would the battering she was enduring now leave her softened but not damaged or would she break under the strain? She thought of her aunt and uncle and Mathew. Would they break under what was to come for them?

Tears came to her eyes at the thought. They didn't deserve this.

PJ knelt and let the piece of pottery go, watching it wash back out to sea. She put her hands down in the sand and felt the water wash over them, burying them bit by bit with each retreating wave.

Gabe had been right. This home he'd found on the Connecticut coastline was the perfect place to escape the world.

She stood, turning to head back toward Gabe's. Twenty yards down the shore, she could make him out standing and waiting for her. She smiled. Had he been there the whole time, watching over her?

It took her a few minutes to meet up with him and when they did, he turned and fell into step beside her.

The silence between them was comfortable and PJ walked by his side for several minutes before saying anything.

"Are you my bodyguard for the week?" She asked. She'd given her real bodyguards the week off, though they were staying in a nearby hotel so they could meet her at a moment's notice if she needed them back on duty.

Gabe brushed her shoulder with his, the connection sparking warmth in her chest.

"Just wanted to be sure you weren't out here alone if anyone recognized you."

She knew how quickly a crowd could converge on her if that did happen. It was rarely one or two people saying hello. It might start like that, but as soon as one person asked for a selfie with her, others would notice and things could get out of hand before she had time to make it back to Gabe's.

"Thank you," she said. "I was thinking I could cook for you tonight."

Gabe raised a brow at her? "Yeah?"

She narrowed her eyes at him. "I can cook. I mean, it's not going to be anything gourmet, but I can make pasta or something."

The amusement in his eyes was a little too clear, but he nodded. "Deal. But feel free to put me to work chopping or making meatballs or whatever you need."

Why did the image of them cooking side-by-side together make her stomach flip over?

Because there was something so normal in that. She realized, then, that's partly what had made these couple of days so great. The normality of it all. Eating on the couch while they watched T.V., waking up in a bed that wasn't in a hotel suite, not having a team of people around her to let her know where she needed to be next or who was waiting for an interview.

She would miss this.

"Meatballs, huh? If you make homemade meatballs, that's totally going to put my pasta and sauce from a jar to shame."

When Gabe caught her hand in his and held it as they walked, it felt natural. Natural and so damned good. Warm and comforting as their palms aligned and they came over the last dune near the gate to his backyard.

"I promise to ooh and ah over your sauce from a jar."

Laughter filled her as she shook her head. "I do make a mean garlic bread if you have any Italian bread."

"No Italian bread, but I think there are some dinner rolls in the freezer. Would those work?"

"As long as I can smear it with way too much butter and sprinkle it with garlic, it'll work."

He held the gate for her and PJ soaked in the night and wished she had more than a week here in this secret hideaway from the world and all her problems. Just a little longer before she had to face reality.

CHAPTER 8

*P*J woke slowly, blinking back the light that streamed in through the gauzy white curtains hanging over the patio doors. Clearing her head of the dream that woke her wasn't easy. Her hand went to her mouth where she could almost feel Gabe's mouth on hers as it had been in her dream.

Last night, they'd eaten dinner without the kiss that had accompanied their burgers the night before. Still, that didn't mean her mind was any further from it than it had been.

She could taste him. Feel him as he had gripped her tight and slanted his mouth over hers, tangling his tongue with hers, taking what he wanted. Giving her what she needed.

She shook off the remnants of the dream and looked around the room as the events of the last few days came back to her. Not the kiss with Gabe, but all the rest of it.

The journal, the Kurt interview. She groaned and rolled over, pulling the covers up over her face. What she wouldn't give to wind back the clock. Except for the kiss...

She felt absolutely wrecked. Never mind the emotional toll of everything that had been happening. There was the fact she and Gabe had stayed up talking all Thursday night. She'd then had a short nap on the plane, but that was hardly enough to catch her up.

Last night, she'd gone to bed early, only to toss and turn the whole night, imagining what Gabe Sawyer could have done with those hands and that mouth, that tongue, if he hadn't put the brakes on that kiss.

Oh, that kiss. Talk about melting her brain and setting her body on fire.

But, Gabe was right. It was the last thing she needed. She cringed at the memory of him stopping the kiss. He'd barely touched her lips and the next thing she knew, she'd practically thrown herself at him, clinging to him.

Ugh. PJ rolled over again and pulled the sheet off her head, staring out at the sun through the drapes. She was mortified at how she'd behaved. He probably thought she was completely trashy. The littlest bit of compassion from a man—of pity, really—and she took that and ran with it, making it into something entirely different.

PJ hated to admit it, but she really was a complete idiot when it came to relationships with men. Her first relationship hadn't even been a real relationship.

And she hadn't had many relationships that were even close to serious since then, unless you count Kurt. And, oh, what a disaster that had been. She'd been fooled once again into thinking he cared for her.

She hadn't been gullible enough to think it was love, *yet.* But, her feelings could have headed that way until she found out he wasn't even remotely headed in the same direction.

PJ's phone beeped on the nightstand, and she looked at the screen as her stomach clenched in a tight knot. She was almost afraid to have any connection to the outside world right now. She forced herself to look anyway, but not before she saw it was a text from Debra.

You need to look at Twitter. We're on top of it, trying to get it shut down and releasing a statement talking about balancing your need for privacy while giving your fans access to you, yada yada. Take a look and we'll touch base with you later.

PJ held her breath as she hit the small bird on her home screen and pulled up Twitter.

Jimmy's Little Whore filled her feed. Those words appeared over and over in what seemed like hundreds of tweets, complete with the hashtag #jimmyswhore. PJ clicked on the link in one of the tweets and was taken to a web page that showed several of her journal entries from her time with Jimmy Mondo.

Everything from the first touches of his hands on her body to the day she lost her virginity. Complete with all of her ramblings about how special she'd been to him, how much he'd loved her.

Of course, now, as an adult, she knew his reputation in the industry was despicable. It wouldn't come as a huge surprise to anyone that she'd slept with him, although her young age at the time would probably shock them. And get him into deep trouble. She'd been fifteen. She couldn't really blame them for calling her a whore.

PJ scrolled to the bottom. There were hundreds of comments. Some supporting her, telling her how much they loved her, and how disgusting he'd been to take advantage of her. Others calling her a slut, saying she'd probably seduced him, speculating about how she'd made her name in the industry, how she'd gotten her big break.

Still more wondered why Jimmy hadn't been arrested, while others were angry that someone would steal her journal and release such private information.

PJ wished she could say she didn't feel ashamed and humiliated. But she did. She hated the idea that people knew what she'd done, how she'd spread her legs at the mere promise of love.

She jumped at the sound of a knock on her door.

"Pru? You awake?" came Gabe's voice softly through the door.

Gabe. PJ squeezed her eyes shut when she realized Gabe

would be reading this stuff this morning, too. Gabe...her parents...Lydia...Ellis. *Ugh.*

"Yeah, I'm up. I'll, um. I'll be out in a minute," she said.

"Okay. No rush. I've got some fruit cut up for breakfast and there's cereal on the counter if you want it. Help yourself to anything. I'm going to head out to the beach for a run."

"Thank you," PJ said, trying to hide the relief in her voice. With the things he'd probably read about her today, she wasn't in any rush to face him.

Her phone beeped and PJ glanced at the screen, afraid she'd see a blocked number again. *Ellis* showed as the Caller ID. She clicked on her messages in case Ellis was passing along important info from either Lydia or Debra, as he often did.

As the lowest person in terms of seniority on the team of people closest to her, he often ended up playing the part of messenger and even gofer, when there wasn't anyone else around.

At times, PJ felt Lydia pushed him around a bit too much, and PJ had talked to Lydia about it a time or two. Ellis was important to the team, whether Lydia wanted to view her brother that way or not.

It was also well known among them all that Ellis had a pretty strong, albeit one-sided, crush on PJ. She was flattered and considered him a friend, but hadn't ever had feelings for him beyond that.

As she opened his messages, she almost regretted there was no spark between them. Ellis was faithful and supportive. He would probably never treat her the way Kurt had, and he certainly would never take advantage of someone so much younger than him the way Jimmy had. Ellis was just, deep down, a really good person. Why couldn't she be attracted to him?

She frowned as images of Gabe filled her mind. His toned and tight body, his eyes as they bored into hers moments before his mouth captured hers.... She was attracted to Gabe Sawyer and she didn't think he was a bad person. She knew he wasn't the type of person to do what Jimmy did.

As for what Kurt had done? She didn't think he'd be unfaithful like Kurt, but that didn't mean he would want anything long term or exclusive. She'd seen enough pictures of him with models and celebrities on his arm to know he dated. A lot.

She also wasn't sure he was what she needed right now. She couldn't say why. Maybe it was just the fact she was so attracted to him that made him seem dangerous, in a way. She was so attracted to him, her veneer of control was slipping away—that couldn't possibly be good for her.

PJ read the string of messages from Ellis.

Are you hanging in there?

You've seen the news this morning, right?

Try to ignore it... They're just trying to mess with your head.

She smiled, but there wasn't much happiness in it. Of course Ellis would support her. He always did. But what did everyone else think? Even if they supported her now, would they still feel the same when they found out the rest of the story?

Thanx, E. I appreciate you! Just trying to rest right now and not pay attention to it until I have to:)

Talk about Queen of Denial.

Another text from Ellis came through.

Kurt keeps calling Lydia. He wants your number but she won't give it to him.

Why would Kurt want to talk to her?

Thanks, she texted quickly, then slid off the bed and went to the kitchen to get something to eat. The last thing she wanted was to talk to Kurt.

She had just picked up an apple when a very angry, almost dangerous-looking Gabe stormed back in the house. His eyes were almost black as he glowered and held his phone out. It showed the website she'd just looked at moments before.

"Is it true?" He all but growled the words at her and PJ

clutched the edges of her robe together. She thought about giving him a vague answer that neither confirmed nor denied, but she knew Gabe wouldn't put up with that.

She straightened her spine and met his eye when she spoke, forcing her words to come out strong and clear. "Yes. It's true."

PJ watched as the muscles in his jaw twitched, and she could see him grinding his teeth together. He looked at her for another minute and she could see the disgust in his eyes.

She didn't look away. She was through letting people judge her. Her whole damn life was being splattered across every social media platform that had been invented. She didn't need him — one of the only people she'd begun to think of as a friend— judging her too.

Before she could think of something to say, Gabe spun on his heel and went back the way he'd come, heading out through the patio doors and back onto the beach. PJ watched him jog down the beach as she sank onto one of the bar stools that lined the kitchen island. She should probably pack her bags and leave, but she didn't know where to go, or how....

She could go to Susie and Brian's. In fact, she probably should try to help them deal with the fallout she was sure would be hitting them soon.

But honestly, she didn't know if they'd want her there. Probably not. They would want to deal with this as a family.

A family.

PJ went back in the house and showered, letting the hot water run down her body in waves, tilting her head back and feeling the water on her face. Maybe she should just go somewhere alone.

She could fly to Europe. Maybe rent a little place in Italy for a couple of days. No, that didn't make sense. She'd end up sitting on a plane for most of her time off, not to mention the thought of going to the airport where she might be recognized sucked.

It wasn't lost to her that she had no true friends to turn to right now. She had her team, and she could always go home to her parents, but with her life on the road the way she was all the time, she didn't have the kind of friendships a person needed at a time like this.

Her team was wonderful and she loved her parents, but that wasn't the same thing as having real friends to lean on. Ellis was younger than PJ, and he wasn't exactly the kind of friend she could turn to for support at a time like this.

In theory, she and Lydia should be close. Their parents had been friends for years and they were only a few years apart in age. Since she'd hired Lydia as her tour manager, they saw each other all the time, but they hadn't ever really bonded.

Lydia was frighteningly ambitious and career oriented. Which was great when she was running PJ's tours, but the control and intensity Lydia needed to pull that off didn't really translate into 'girlfriend' material.

PJ could rent a car and drive to that little spa she'd once gone to in upstate New York. That shouldn't be too far from here and they could probably fit her in if she called ahead. They had been great about respecting her privacy the last time. It wouldn't be a bad place to go to stick her head in the sand.

She squeezed her eyes shut at the thought of having to go back on tour, even if it was almost a week away. PJ swallowed and thought again about walking away from it all.

She'd been thinking a lot about that lately. About just going out while she was still on top. And now the thought seemed to take hold more firmly in her head than ever before. Earlier, it had just been an occasional note in her journal, quickly dismissed when she thought of her fans.

But, now. Well, now things were different. Usually, if she got down or stressed out, she could work on her music, get out her keyboard or guitar and write something new. Or tweak something old.

Not in the last few days, though. She felt as though all the music had drained out of her. She didn't have anything left to give. And, she hated that defeated feeling—it wasn't something she was used to.

PJ turned off the water and stepped from the shower, taking a deep breath and telling herself to stop the pity party. It wasn't anything but the truth coming out now. She needed to deal with the choices she'd made when she was young: the choice to get into bed with Jimmy Mondo, the decision to give up her baby.

There wasn't anything to it other than that. It was simply time for her to deal with the mistakes of her past.

Gabe dragged himself back to the house. He'd run a lot further than his usual three miles, trying like hell to get the images of Jimmy Mondo seducing a much-too-young PJ, out of his head. What the hell had her parents been thinking about, not pressing charges?

The man had essentially raped Pru, plying her with alcohol. Gabe had a feeling it was most likely Jimmy who had gotten her hooked on alcohol in the first place. That man should have been strung up – not walking around representing other artists.

Strung up. That's what Gabe wanted to do to him. Hunt him down and tie him up by the balls and leave him to him rot. He stopped just before the back doors and took a few deep breaths.

He had to get ahold of himself before he saw Pru. He opened the French doors and stepped into the kitchen just as she stepped out of her bedroom, carrying her bag.

"What's wrong, Pru? Where are you going?" Gabe said, watching an almost guilty look wash over her features.

She fidgeted and crossed her arms over her chest. "I'm just gonna get out of your hair, Gabe. I'm going to call for a rental car and drive to a spa for a couple of days." She looked down at her toes as she spoke and Gabe hated to see her so fragile. So alone.

"Hey." He stepped closer and put a hand to her cheek, brushing her face until she looked up at him. "I don't want you to go, Pru. I want you to stay here so we can fix this together."

Her eyes were like giant saucers looking back at him as if she couldn't believe he wanted her to stay. "But, you...you seemed so angry with me this morning. And, there was that kiss that made things weird...." She let her voice trail off.

Gabe felt like he'd been kicked in the gut. He hadn't realized PJ would think he was mad at her this morning. How could she not know he'd be mad at what had been done to her, not mad at her? He wanted to step closer, pull her into his arms and breathe in the sweet scent of her skin.

But, he forced himself not to do that to her. God, this woman had been dealing with people taking advantage of her all her life. He didn't want her to think he was trying to add to that list.

"I wasn't angry with you," he said shaking his head. "How could I ever be angry with you for what that..." He felt the bitter taste of hatred and disgust on his tongue at the thought of Jimmy Mondo. "What that *asshole* did to you. He took advantage of you, Pru. Manipulated and used you when he should have been protecting you. You were fifteen for Christ's sake."

"You were so angry when you left here."

He dropped his head, looking down as he realized how that had looked to her when he ran out that morning. "Not at you, Pru. Never at you."

PJ tilted her face up to meet his eyes. "So it's okay if I stay?"

"Of course. How else are we going to solve this problem if you don't stay and help me?" he asked.

"This isn't your problem to fix." PJ shook her head at him.

He ignored her objection. "The first step is tracking down your ex-manager. We need to see if there's any way to bring charges against him now—and if there isn't, I'll take care of him myself."

"No, Gabe!" PJ said, a lot more sharply this time, and he could hear the desperation in her voice. What the hell was she trying to hide, and why?

It was stupid, but Gabe actually felt hurt that she wouldn't open up to him, or trust him, with whatever she was hiding. But really, why should she? They didn't know each other all that well.

"You can't do that, Gabe. You need to leave this alone——"

"Are you crazy, Pru? Your parents should have pressed charges against him a long time ago! They should never have let him walk away like they did," Gabe spit out, and he knew he was doing a piss-poor job of hiding his frustration.

PJ took a deep breath. "Look, I appreciate what you're trying to do, but you have to trust me on this. The time for going after Jimmy is long past. I'm over what happened and I don't want to bring it up again. Well...." She blew out a rough breath—half laugh, half groan. "Not any more than it's already been dredged up for the world to see."

Gabe opened his mouth to object but she cut him off.

"No. Listen, please." She softened her tone. "I need you to leave this alone for me. Please?" Her phone beeped again and PJ glanced at the screen. She went stark white, and Gabe didn't miss the little intake of breath.

"What is it?" he asked.

PJ stammered her response. "N-nothing. Just my manager arranging more interviews for me when I get back. PR, damage control, that kind of thing," she said weakly and shoved her phone in her back pocket.

She was lying. There was no way texts from her manager would bring that reaction—at least they shouldn't— not even if they were texts about scheduling interviews PJ didn't want to do. He crossed his arms and eyed her, but she remained committed to the lie.

"Will you at least let me help you figure out who's got your journal so we can stop them from releasing anything else?"

Her teeth sank into her lower lip as she thought about it. "I don't really see what you can do to help with that. I mean, there's not really any way to figure that out, is there?"

"Well, you could start by telling me the truth about who just texted you and why they're texting," he said, trying one more time to get her to open up to him.

Nope. He watched her face shut down and go completely blank.

"I told you. It was Debra."

Gabe ground his teeth together again. He'd been doing a lot of that the last few days. He purposefully loosened his jaw and shrugged a shoulder.

"Fine. Why don't I make us a little something more substantial for breakfast and you can throw your stuff back in your room. We'll be heading over to Jack's for the party at three, if that's okay with you," he said.

The look of relief on PJ's face when he dropped the subject had him worried. *What the hell is she hiding?*

He watched as she went to her room and shut the door, then stepped down the hall to his own room to change clothes. Once locked away in his room, he dialed Chad.

Chad Thompson was the head of Security and Investigations for Sutton Capital. If anyone could find the origin of the content of those texts coming to PJ's phone, Chad would be the one to do it.

"Hey, Gabe!" came Chad's voice on the other end of the phone. "You in town for the party?"

"Yeah, I am. I'll see you guys later today. I assume you and Jennie and the baby will be there?"

Chad laughed. "Kelly and Jennie would both string me up if I missed it. I think they're having pony rides for the kids."

Gabe shook his head. Leave it to Jack to have pony rides for a two-year-old's birthday party.

"Listen," Gabe said and lowered his voice. "I need a favor. If I give you a cell phone number, can you see texts coming into that phone without me handing you the phone physically?"

Chad groaned. "Do I want to know what this is about?"

Gabe hesitated a minute before speaking.

"It's Pru. She's in trouble, but she won't tell me what's going on." He didn't have to explain who Pru was. Chad and Jack and Andrew all knew Gabe was more than a little infatuated with PJ Cantrell, and that he still called her by her pre-fame nickname of Pru. It was how she'd first introduced herself to him and it had stuck.

"What kind of trouble?" Chad asked.

"I really don't know for sure. Have you caught any of what's going on in the news?"

"Jennie said she'd been having a tough time lately. Something about rumors and leaks," Chad said.

"It's pretty bad. Someone has her journal, and they're posting all kinds of personal stuff about her on the Internet and leaking similar things to the tabloids. But, I think there's more to it than she's telling me. She's getting texts that seem to have her reeling, but she won't tell me what they're about or who they're from."

Chad was quiet for a long time before answering. "Is she there with you at the house?"

"Yeah. She's coming to the party later."

"If I can get hold of her phone at some point during the party, I'll duplicate her SIM card and put it in a blank phone for you so you can see what's coming in. If we can't get hold of her phone, I'll have to load some software onto your phone and then, provided you're both within range of the same cell tower and she isn't having messages encrypted, you'll be able to read them on your phone."

"Thanks, Chad. I owe you one."

"Shoot, you owe me a lot more than that. This is extraordinarily illegal and pretty damn immoral. Are you sure you want to spy on the woman you want a relationship with? This is beginning to feel stalker-ish," Chad said.

"I can't have a relationship with her if she's not safe. I'm sure someone's threatening her, Chad. I can tell from her reaction to these texts. I want to keep her safe, and if that means giving up a shot at a relationship with her, so be it."

Chad was quiet for a long moment before grunting his agreement and hanging up the phone.

Gabe steeled himself against the guilt creeping into his gut as he remembered the kiss the night before. He went to the kitchen to make some breakfast. He needed to focus on PJ's safety right now. Nothing else.

CHAPTER 9

*P*J stared at the words that came through on her phone display moments before.

Pretty Pru? Are you having a good morning now that the world knows you're a whore? Whores who spread their legs have to pay the price someday, Pretty Pru. Or did you plan to lie to the world forever? Did you think you could hide what you truly are from everyone?

Anger flashed hot and strong through PJ, past the fear and panic she was feeling. Who was this person and what reason did they have to do this to her?

What do you want? Why are you doing this? She typed and sent the text back.

It was a long time before a response came back, and she had begun to wonder if the person would even answer her.

I want the world to know the truth. To know how much you've lied to everyone all these years. But, if I think you've paid your debt and are truly repentant, perhaps I won't tell your final secret.

PJ waited but nothing more came. She threw her phone across the room. Not hard enough to damage it, but enough for a satisfying *thunk* to sound through the room. She walked from the room without picking it up.

She should have turned it off after watching the third interview Kurt Tollison had done since the news of her and Jimmy broke. He was getting more than a little mileage out of this whole thing.

At least, he'd been sympathetic to her in his interviews. He put on his best serious face and told people he was wrecked by the news. No, she hadn't ever told him. Yes, he would have supported her if he'd known what happened.

Because he was such a good guy like that.

Lydia had let PJ know Kurt had reached out again, wanting her phone number. He said he wanted to call and let PJ know he was there for her.

It wasn't hard to imagine how Erika would react to him trying to get in touch with PJ. She'd always been so threatened by PJ and the idea that Kurt might go back to her.

It always made PJ's head spin to think about women who dated someone who'd cheated like that. Who would want a man who had cheated on someone else to be with you? You'd have to be an idiot not to realize if they did it with you, they would do it again.

Gabe and PJ walked across the back lawn and through the wooden gate in the stone wall that split Jack and Kelly's property from Gabe's. PJ felt almost wistful at the idea of living so close to such good friends. Of course, Gabe didn't live here full time. His life was almost as much in motion as hers. But, at least he seemed to be starting to put down some roots. She had no stability anywhere in sight, but the more she saw of the life Gabe was beginning to build for himself here, the more she thought about making changes in her own life.

"So, if you do end up selling your hotels, is this where you'll come? You'll live here full time?" PJ asked as they walked up Jack and Kelly's lawn toward the back of the house.

"Yeah. I think so. I like it here and I have more ties here than anywhere else," he answered, pulling her hand into his.

"What about your family?" she asked. She realized they'd never talked about his family. She had no idea if he had brothers or sisters or was close to his parents, but she didn't miss the sadness in his eyes at her question.

"My mom's in a home about an hour from here. She needs round-the-clock care," he said.

PJ squeezed his hand and he continued.

"My dad and sister died in a car accident when I was in college. It was the day before my sister's high school graduation and my mom.... She just never really recovered from that."

PJ shook her head. "I don't know how anyone could recover from that," she said and his eyes met hers.

Her breath caught at the intensity of the look in his eyes, but then the moment passed, as quickly as it had come and she felt Gabe break the connection.

PJ was about to press him further, but he laughed and pointed across the lawn, clearly not wanting to talk about his family anymore. She wanted to tell him how sorry she was, but would the words really offer any comfort? Most likely just letting him drop the conversation would be best.

"Not only did Jack get Maddie pony rides for her birthday, he's got a bouncy castle and jugglers. Man, what will he do when she turns three? Or sixteen?"

PJ laughed and looked across the lawn at the large spread before them. There were kids and adults everywhere, some jumping and playing in the pool, others fisting cupcakes and hot dogs. Apparently, they weren't going to wait until the birthday song had been sung to dig into the sweets. PJ grinned. She wouldn't mind a cupcake.

Gabe's thumb moved back and forth over her hand and she felt her stomach jump. He'd made it clear the other night that he didn't want anything more than friendship but apparently the jumping beans in her stomach hadn't gotten the hint.

She was hyperaware of how she looked, what she was wearing, and whether he might find her attractive. Enough so that she had a hard time focusing when several of the guests made their way over and introductions were made.

She tried to remember if it was Andrew and Jill who lived up the street, or Chad and Jennie. Jennie held a beautiful baby girl who twisted in her arms, reaching for the ground.

"Okay, Ella," Jennie said as she put the little girl on the ground and watched her crawl into the soft grass of the large backyard. "Run amok, baby girl."

Then there were Jesse and Zach and Jack and Kelly. With all the Js, PJ felt sure she'd get something wrong and mix them up. But Gabe stayed with her the whole time, and made more introductions and included her in the conversations.

His friends were welcoming, too. Once she'd sorted out in her head who was who, she enjoyed seeing them all catch up with Gabe and fill him in on their lives since he'd been back for his last visit a few months before.

"How are things at the bakery, Jesse?" one of the women asked. PJ was almost certain it was Jill. Or maybe it was Kelly. No, Kelly was chasing the adorable birthday girl who was currently screeching, "Mine! Mine!" and indiscriminately pointing to all of the toys, ponies and the bouncy castle.

"It's been really great. We had the soft opening for people in the office building about three months ago and then the grand opening for the public a week later." Jesse smiled. "I had a couple employees that just didn't seem to get that we needed to treat the customers as though we wanted them there, but they've been replaced and things have been running smoothly ever since."

"That's great. It must be so exciting to see it all coming together," Jill said and then turned to PJ. "Jesse owns a bakery in the lobby of the building where Sutton Capital is located."

PJ smiled. "Oh, that's exciting. Is that how you guys know each other?" She was still trying to match up all the connections between the friends.

Andrew, Chad and Jack worked together. Chad and Jack were also cousins. But, she hadn't quite figured out where Jesse and Zach fit in.

Jesse laughed and shook her head. "I'm Kelly's older sister. Jack gave me the bakery as a gift." Her grin got wider as PJ's eyebrows rose.

"I know. Some gift, huh? It was mostly a bribe. I had, uh, a little trouble going out of the house and feeling safe for a while after Kelly was kidnapped. I had to put my dream of going to pastry school on hold. Jack eventually hired Zach to be my bodyguard, gave me the bakery, sent me to school and, well, pretty much fixed my world."

Zach's arms linked around Jesse as she spoke and he pulled her back into him. PJ smiled.

She had known Kelly had been kidnapped. Gabe told her about it shortly after it happened during one of their rooftop talks. She had no idea Jesse had developed anxiety issues because of it. Seeing the couple now, though, it looked like it might have been a blessing in disguise.

Jill's phone chimed and she excused herself from the group to take the call. The chatter amongst the friends continued until Jill came back, looking visibly shaken.

"What is it?" Andrew asked, crossing to take her hand. Jill tilted her head up at him.

"That was the agency. They have a baby for us. Well, no.... They have two. Twins. Twin boys. They're in a hospital in Houston, and the birth mother is ready to give up her rights, but we have to decide right away if we're okay with twins."

PJ's stomach bottomed out as the topic of birth mothers and adoption was discussed. Within minutes, Jill and Andrew were surrounded by Kelly, Jack, Chad, Jennie and even Jack's house-keeper, Mrs. Poole.

"We're not even remotely prepared for twins, Andrew." Jill all but whispered the words, and it was clear she was uncertain, but hope and excitement were also evident in her expression.

"We'll get you guys ready before you can even get those babies back here," Kelly said, not missing a beat—Jennie and Jesse nodded.

"We can shop for doubles of everything," Jesse said. "We'll just match what you already chose and buy a second."

Jennie spoke up. "And we can rework the nursery or move it to one of the bigger rooms if you need us to. That larger guest room on the other side of the master bedroom would work well for two babies. We can paint in there and have it finished before you get back."

It seemed as if the group held a collective breath. Andrew looked down at Jill, who stood biting her lip. "I'm game, if you are," he said and the grin on his face was wide and easy.

"Oh, thank heavens," Jill said as she sagged against him with relief.

"Jill?"

"Yeah?" she answered, her voice muffled against his chest.

"You already told them yes, didn't you?" Andrew asked with a laugh, and the rest of the group laughed with him when Jill nodded her head against his chest.

"I'll take care of the flight," Kelly said turning toward the house. Mrs. Poole followed, letting them know she'd book a hotel.

"Call the Towers, Mrs. Poole. Let them know to reserve a room for an open-ended stay for my friends. The manager there is Paul Grandon. He'll set everything up," Gabe said.

She called out a thank you over her shoulder as Jill explained that she and Andrew would likely have to be in Houston for at least two weeks, and possibly longer if the twins needed further care. They were in the NICU at the moment because they were born four weeks premature, but the agency had said that no major complications were expected at this time.

As PJ watched the group, feeling like an outsider, she was struck by how quickly and easily all of them pulled together to help when Jill and Andrew needed them. She suspected any of their friends would get the same treatment if they found themselves in need of support. But, it also made her realize that some of her decisions thirteen years ago hadn't been wrong.

Yes, she'd slept with a man she had no business being with, and she'd done it at an age when she was far too young to take responsibility for the outcome of their actions. But the choices she'd made since then were all good ones.

As soon as she'd found out she was pregnant, she had gone to her parents. She quit drinking, and she'd made the heart-wrenching decision to put her baby up for adoption. Whoever it was that was tormenting her now, whoever had her journal.... They were wrong. She didn't need to pay for that decision. It had been the right one.

Watching Jill and Andrew and the love that already shone in their eyes for two babies they had yet to meet, it was clear. Sometimes adoption *was* the right choice. These twins would have a wonderful life with loving parents. They would be safe and cherished and loved.

And Matthew had been given a wonderful life with her Aunt Susie and Uncle Brian. Letting them adopt Matthew had been the best decision she'd ever made. Whoever her tormenter was, he had asked if she thought her baby cried himself to sleep at night and how she felt about that.

And, she'd let it get to her. Briefly. But no longer. She knew Matthew had never been without Brian and Susie's love and care. She knew he had a better life than she could ever have given him as a teenage mom.

Her gut still clenched at the thought of that information

getting out, though. They hadn't told Matthew she was his birth mother yet. He knew he was adopted, but he thought she was just his cousin. She didn't want this person to force Brian and Susie to tell him before they were ready to—before Matthew was ready to hear it.

And she didn't want to even think about the changes that would come to his stable life if that information was released before they were ready. He'd be hounded by the paparazzi and thrust into the limelight right after receiving the shock of a lifetime.

No, she thought. She couldn't let that happen. She'd do anything, pay anything, to stop the truth from getting out.

CHAPTER 10

*G*abe watched for any chance to slip PJ's phone away from her, but she kept it in her pocket the whole time they were at Jack's. Toward the end of the party, he slipped away and grabbed Chad.

"I haven't been able to get her phone. You said there's something you can upload to my phone?" Gabe reminded Chad when they were alone in Jack's home office.

"Sure. I need to load some firmware onto your phone, but you're still going to have to find out what carrier she uses for her cell service, and it will only work when you guys are within range of the same base tower." Chad took Gabe's phone and attached it to Jack's computer with a USB cable, then put in the password to unlock the computer. "You sure you want to do this?"

Gabe nodded, his jaw set. If she wouldn't tell him what was going on, he'd find out. No way was she dealing with this on her own.

Chad rolled his eyes and mumbled something about 'dumber than a post' under his breath, but his fingers began flying over the keys as he pulled up whatever illegal firmware he needed to make this happen. When he'd finished, he pulled the cord out of the phone and handed it back to Gabe.

"Call me when you find out what carrier she uses and I'll walk you through the rest."

Gabe ignored the guilt needling him and went back out to find PJ.

Later that night, a casual question about possibly changing his cell phone carrier got Gabe the information he needed. The following morning, he read the first of PJ's text messages for the day. He wasn't able to see the texts she'd gotten prior to that point. And so far that day, all she'd received was a text from Ellis checking to see how she was doing.

Gabe had met Ellis once or twice. He wasn't a very memorable guy, but since he was part of PJ's team, Gabe had made a point to remember him. He was small and mousy, often taking way too much crap from Lydia, but he was fiercely loyal to PJ. Gabe had to give him that.

PJ texted back that she was fine. Just trying to relax.

Gabe slid his phone under his chair on the patio when he saw PJ open her bedroom door and walk toward him through the kitchen.

"I thought maybe we'd go out on the boat today," Gabe said, smiling at her.

"I didn't pack a bathing suit," PJ said glancing toward the dock where his sailboat bobbed lazily on the water.

"I've got extras. I'm sure I can find something horribly skimpy that'll let me get cheap thrills all day," he said and grinned at her.

Playing with fire, jackass. For whatever reason, Gabe couldn't stop himself from feeding the sexual tension between them. Not that it really needed to be fed. It was alive and kicking and doing quite well on its own.

He watched her face flush with heat and smiled to know he'd put that color there. She had been even quieter than usual after the party yesterday, and he wanted to find a way to put a smile back on her face, and keep it there for a while if he could.

When they stepped onto his boat an hour later—picnic

basket, towels and sunscreen in hand—she still looked tense and stressed. He hoped he could get her to relax and forget what was happening on Facebook and Twitter. He'd been checking social media sites all day and the journal entries had gone viral.

Everyone had an opinion, but he was glad to see there was a huge chunk of people supporting her. A lot of people realized what happened with her former manager wasn't her fault. The blame should be put at *his* feet, not hers.

But, the stress of the situation was evident on PJ's face. He stowed the picnic basket under one of the bench seats, then grabbed two bottles of water. They left the dock and set sail once PJ had settled in.

She seemed content to sit quietly, her face turned to the morning sun as he raised the sails. His boat was small enough to allow him to handle himself, and he had them skimming over the open water in no time.

He'd always loved the way the wind hit his face, the slight tinge of the salt mixing with the sun relaxed him like nothing else could. Maybe it could do the same for her.

When he reached their destination in a quiet cove, Gabe lowered the anchor over the side of the boat, grabbed their picnic basket and sank down onto the seat across from her. He wanted to sit next to her.

Hell, he wanted to pull her into his lap and devour those lips that had been driving him mad since the kiss they shared a few nights ago. He couldn't get the taste of her, the feel of her, out of his head. He wanted more of her. A lot more.

But, he'd settle for talking to her for now. Maybe someday, down the road.... It occurred to him that he'd been saying that for a long time where PJ was concerned. But he had to be brutally honest, now really wasn't a good time for her. Her world was crumbling. She didn't need him hitting on her right now.

He would hate it if she thought he assumed she was easy because he'd seen all the reports of her sleeping with Mondo.

That she'd have no problem putting out for him the way she did with Jimmy. The thought made him wince.

"So, when was the last time you took a vacation?" he asked her as he unwrapped the sandwiches and handed one to her.

She smiled, and the warmth of it cut through him. "Not for years, really. It was a complete fluke to have six days off like this. And, even when I have had time off recently, I haven't gone anywhere except back home every once in a while."

"What family do you have back home?" he asked.

"My parents, and my Aunt Susie and Uncle Brian and their son Matthew." Gabe thought he saw a little bit of a cloud fall over her face at the mention of her family, but it disappeared as quickly as it had shown up, and he wasn't sure if maybe he'd just imagined it. She took a bite of her sandwich and a swallow of water.

"Do you still have a lot of friends back home?" he asked.

"A few," she said, but her face was sad again. "Nothing like the friendships you guys have here. It was really amazing to see how quickly everybody gathered around Jill and Andrew yesterday. How everyone jumped in to help them without any hesitation at all."

"You don't have friends who would do that for you?" Gabe asked and then wanted to kick himself as soon as the words were out.

PJ hesitated. "Honestly? I'm not sure anymore. It's not easy making friends out on the road, and the friends I had back when I started my career have such different lives now. I was fifteen when I left to go on tour. They have husbands and families. They're on a completely different path than I'm on."

Gabe nodded. He knew exactly what she meant. He'd been watching his friends build lives here while he was out on the road, stopping in from time to time. If it was possible, he was pretty sure PJ traveled even more than he did.

"Do you think you'll want to retire soon?" he asked.

PJ brushed her hair back from her face and looked back out toward the water. "I've thought about it some lately. Honestly? I just don't know what I want to do anymore. You know? I usually have songs playing in my head, things I'm working on. I haven't heard anything there for three days. It's like the music has just stopped playing in my head, and it makes me wonder if maybe there's just some... expiration date. Maybe I've hit mine."

"You started pretty young and you've had a long career already," Gabe said. "Do you think you want to do something else? Manage other singers? Start a family?"

Again, he saw the shadow fall over her face, and he had to wonder if she wanted a family more than she let on. She never did answer his question. She stared out at the water and was quiet the rest of the ride back as he packed up lunch, caught some wind in the sails and brought them back to the dock.

Gabe held out his hand to her as they stepped off the boat and then held it all the way up to the house. PJ knew she shouldn't do it, but she couldn't help it. She couldn't help wanting to kiss Gabe again, even after his rejection the last time. She didn't want to be trapped inside her head, obsessing over who had her journal and whether they would ever release all the truth or just make her suffer forever. She didn't want to feel the way she was feeling anymore.

She tugged at Gabe's hand, pulling him back to face her when they reached the patio.

He turned, a question in his eyes, but she just wrapped her arms around his neck and pulled him down close, close enough that when she stood on her tiptoes she could reach his mouth.

She let her fingers thread through his hair as she brushed her lips against his, and heard him drop the picnic basket next to them.

He let out a fierce groan as she deepened the kiss, but he didn't kiss her back. *Please, please don't reject me.* She knew she couldn't handle his rejection now. She didn't care if it was a pity screw or just friends with benefits, or whatever.

But, she knew she wanted to be closer to him—to escape. To feel something else right now. To feel him. His hands on her. His mouth on her. *Him* inside her.

Gabe broke away and looked at her, heat and desire smoldering in his eyes, but she also saw confusion, conflict. "Are you sure, Pru? You don't have to do this for me. I don't need this from you. Not now."

"But I do," she said. "*I* need this from you."

She had only just gotten the words out of her mouth before he pulled her against him, assaulting her mouth with his as if he'd been waiting, tethered—dying to be released. As though she'd just cut the last rope that bound him.

He controlled everything about their kiss, lifting her off the ground and walking through the house as his mouth traveled down her neck and across her shoulders. PJ's body was on fire as his mouth explored her, and she no longer had a thought or a care in her head. She had only this. This moment. This feeling. This escape.

This incredible, desperate escape.

Gabe nudged his bedroom door open and brought her to the bed. He lowered her down, his own body following to press her into the bed with his weight. The feel of him on top of her was everything in that moment—and she reveled in it.

In her heart she knew she couldn't hang on to this beyond today, or maybe tomorrow. Even as he kissed her passionately, she knew that when it was time to go back to her real life, she'd need to let him go. But, she wanted this. She wanted today and tomorrow. Consequences be damned.

Gabe pulled back from her and trailed his hands down her sides, letting his fingers graze the side of her breasts, then along her rib cage, down her hips. The fire that burned through her settled tight and achy between her legs, and she wanted him to slow down and speed up all at once.

"God, you feel incredible, Pru." His voice was ragged with need and PJ pressed her hips up toward him, wanting him to touch more. She wanted him to take off the scraps of fabric he called a bikini and put his hands and mouth on her *there*.

Then she heard a faraway voice calling to her and felt someone shaking her arm.

Leave me alone. As soon as she thought the words, she wondered why on earth someone would be in the bedroom with her and Gabe. But, the words came again. "Pru...? Wake up, Pru."

PJ opened her eyes. Gabe was shaking her awake on the boat. She looked into his dark brown eyes and had a quick flash of panic, as she wondered if she'd been moaning and writhing in her sleep, just as she'd moaned and writhed in her dream. She felt a flush creep up her cheeks, but he didn't bat an eye. Just smiled at her.

"We're back at the dock, Pru. You fell asleep, so I figured we should head in so you can rest in your bed where you'll be more comfortable. Then, maybe we can throw a hat and sunglasses on you and head out for dinner somewhere in town." He spoke easily, so she figured maybe she'd kept the content of her dreams under wraps as she slept.

"Sounds good," she said, sitting up and slipping her flip flops back on her feet. She tried to push the image of Gabe, above her in his bed, out of her mind. She couldn't even look him in the eye as they stood and he helped her climb from the boat.

The way he took her hand in his was too close to the way her dream began. PJ pulled her hand from his as soon as her feet hit the dock. She kept her head down as they walked up to the house and then took his suggestion to go to her room to nap.

Just as she was about to get up and take a shower, her phone rang. PJ picked it up and felt her stomach clench at the sight of a number she didn't know on her screen. She closed her eyes as she answered, though she didn't really know what she hoped to accomplish by doing that.

"Hello?" she said cautiously.

"You little tramp. Who the hell do you think you are? Is this a publicity stunt, PJ? Your career was drying up so you thought you'd go for sympathy?" She knew the voice.

It was the same cold, angry tone Jimmy Mondo had used on her years before when he'd told her to abort their baby. To take care of the mess she'd made, as he'd put it.

PJ disconnected the call, and with shaky hands, turned off her phone. She couldn't keep it off long. Not if there was a chance the guy with her journal would text with his demands. His last texts implied there was something she could do to redeem herself in his eyes or some amount of money she could pay to keep her secret.

Hopefully, Jimmy would quickly get over his need to scream at her, and she could turn her phone back on to wait for the demands from her blackmailer.

She rolled over on her side and pulled her knees up to her chest, hugging herself tightly. She wanted, more than anything, to tell someone what was going on, but who could she tell? Her parents had dealt with too much already. She had told her aunt and uncle, but they needed to help Matthew through this, not worry about her. And, she didn't begrudge them that. She wanted their focus to be on Matthew.

Could she tell Gabe? She thought about it, but she'd hate to see the disappointment, the judgment she was sure would show in his face when she told him. She just couldn't take censure like that right now. Especially from him. Instead, she closed her eyes and tried to forget that she'd stupidly written everything down and by doing so, had opened herself up to this kind of attack.

CHAPTER 11

Gabe stepped out of the shower two hours later. An hour and a half run on the beach and a half hour under the cold spray of the shower had done nothing to relieve his rock-hard erection. An erection he'd had since watching PJ moan and gasp in her sleep on the boat that morning.

He'd never seen a sexier sight in his life. In fact, he'd thought for a minute he could stand there watching her forever, but then he'd realized if he had to watch one more minute, listen to one more of those tiny whimpers coming from her kissable little mouth, he would have stripped her out of that bikini in a heartbeat.

He'd spent half his run trying to forget those sounds, and the other half trying to figure out who she might have been dreaming of. *Jimmy Mondo?* That made sense. She'd been reminded of her history with Jimmy just that morning. Maybe all this had triggered sensuous memories.

But no, that didn't make sense. The look on her face when she'd talked about Jimmy had been one of revulsion, not attraction. Gabe grimaced as he toweled off and drew his jeans up over his hips. Though he looked forward to more time with her, he was in for one hell of an uncomfortable night out with PJ. Every minute with her was torture. He probably shouldn't have invited her along for this trip.

Because you care about her, asshole, and she was hurting. It was as simple as that. What it really came down to was that he cared about her. Gabe grabbed his phone and pulled up the software Chad had installed. *What the hell?*

Dozens of texts going to PJ's number.

You fucking whore, you can't do this to me.

I'll destroy you.

Gabe saw red as he continued to read.

You think you can get away with this? We had an agreement, bitch.

The texts went on and on, threatening PJ and using some language even Gabe wasn't comfortable with—and that said a lot.

He threw open the door to his room and crossed to PJ's door before he realized what he was doing. If he went in there and demanded answers the way he wanted to, he'd have to explain how he knew she was getting those texts. Gabe fisted his hands in his hair and whirled away from her door.

His office. *Chad.* He needed to get Chad on this.

When he'd closed the door, he dialed Chad's number.

"'Lo?" came Chad's voice.

"She's getting some insanely threatening texts, Chad. Any chance you can trace them?"

"Well, hello to you too, Gabe," Chad said cheerfully, but Gabe could hear Chad's fingers on the keyboard and knew Chad wasn't taking this lightly.

Gabe waited until Chad spoke again.

"Is the number blocked or can you see it?"

Gabe pulled his phone away from his ear and pulled up the texts that had gone to PJ's phone. He jotted down the number and put the phone back to his ear before rattling the numbers off to Chad.

"Huh. This guy must not be worried about being traced," Chad said.

"That doesn't make a whole lot of sense if it's the guy who has her journal," Gabe said.

He heard the sound of more typing and then a grunt from Chad. "That's because it's Jimmy Mondo."

"Mondo can't be the person who leaked those parts of her journal, so that must mean she's got two big problems to deal with here," Gabe said, not liking the fact that PJ was keeping all of this so quiet.

Sure, it's not like he was her best friend, but damn, he thought she knew she could come to him for help.

"Have any other texts come through?" Chad asked.

"Not since you installed the software. If the guy who's got the journal has contacted her, it hasn't been since last night."

"Call when you get something and I'll see if I can trace it. If they block the number, there's a possibility I can still get an ID. It all depends on the carrier they use. But, let me know and I'll try," Chad said.

"Thanks, Chad. I owe you," Gabe said. Chad just laughed and hung up the phone.

When Gabe came out of the office, PJ stood at the kitchen island filling a kettle, then placing it on the stove to heat.

"Sorry. I hope you don't mind," she said gesturing to the mug and teapot by the stove.

"Not at all," Gabe said. "Help yourself to anything while you're here. I have the caretakers keep the place pretty heavily stocked." He slid onto a stool across from her and looked at her.

Her eyes still looked tired even though her hair was mussed from bed. She looked like she might have taken a short nap, but didn't get the sleep she needed. Chances were, she wasn't sleeping very well.

"Have you heard from Jimmy Mondo about all this?" he asked, and she damn near jumped out of her skin.

"Um," she started, fidgeting with the handle of her mug.

"If you lie to me, I can't help you," Gabe said quietly. Her round eyes found his and she flushed.

"I don't think there's anything you can do to help me," she whispered, and he wondered why she took on all this by herself.

"What if all I want to do is listen?" he asked though he wanted to tear the guy to pieces. He also wanted to know what had her so scared. And what had Jimmy Mondo so angry? *Could there be more?*

What could be in the journal that hadn't already been leaked?

PJ's eyes seemed locked to his as if she couldn't pull herself away, and he hoped she'd see that all he wanted to do was help. If she'd just open up to him....

The sound of her phone chiming broke the moment and PJ froze, eyeing her phone on the counter as if it were a snake. Gabe's fingers itched to pull out his phone to read the text, but that obviously wasn't an option.

He waited as PJ slowly reached out and read the text, then raised her eyes to his.

"Care to share, Pru?" he asked, and was a bit surprised when she slid the phone across the granite counter to him, her hand shaking the slightest bit. He kept his eyes on hers for just a minute before lifting the phone.

Jimmy doesn't seem at all repentant. How about you, Pretty Pru? Are you ready to repent for your sins?

Ice cold hit Gabe's veins followed by the heat of anger. Burning hot rage because someone was holding something over PJ. And, dammit, she'd been hiding this threat from him the entire time. That needed to change. Now.

Gabe stood, took her hand and pulled PJ over to the living room and settled them onto the couch. Then he faced her. She looked about ready to cry, but he also saw that look of determination beneath the tears that welled in her eyes – like she was gearing up her defenses. He pushed one of her russet curls behind her ear.

"Please, Pru. Let me help. Even if it's just to listen," he said and rubbed a thumb over her cheek where a tear had fallen. "I know you don't want to go to your parents, but you have to have someone on your side through this."

She shook her head. "If I tell you, it will change the way you look at me, how you think about me," she whispered, and he watched as she struggled to control the shaking of her chin, to keep the tears from falling.

"Oh, babe," he leaned his forehead against hers and threaded his fingers through her hair. "Nothing you tell me will ever change the way I see you, or how much I care about you. I promise."

She curled in toward him and he wrapped his arms around her, pulling her close until she almost sat in his lap. It took a long time, but when she began to talk, the words tumbled out of her as if she'd waited years to tell someone her story.

"I didn't spend eight months in rehab," she said against his chest, and Gabe had to make a conscious effort not to stiffen. "I spent two months in rehab. When I checked in, I was two months pregnant."

Well, hell. It was a lot harder not to stiffen for that one, but he steadied his breathing and kept holding her, all the while planning Jimmy Mondo's death in gruesome and excruciating detail in his head.

He'd need to talk to Chad about how to hide a body—he was pretty sure Chad knew that sort of thing. It was good to have friends who would help you bury the bodies.

"Where were you the rest of the time?" he asked. It was widely believed PJ had spent eight months in rehab back when she was fifteen.

"I stayed with my aunt and uncle and my parents. The only time I ever left the house was to go to the doctor."

"And, the baby?" he asked, having a feeling he knew the answer already.

"My cousin, Matthew--" she started, and Gabe finished for her.

"Isn't your cousin."

"No," she said, still not looking up at him.

Gabe tilted her chin to him, bringing her eyes up so he could see them, then dried her tears. He leaned in slowly and kissed her gently on the lips. Such a small kiss, but it seared right through him, just as any contact with her did.

He kissed the tip of her nose, her eyelids and then her lips again before pulling her back down into his arms. She laid her head on his chest and he held her.

"Do you believe you did the right thing? For him? For you?" he asked her.

She pulled back and looked at him. "Yes, I do."

"Do you regret the decision?" he asked.

"Not one bit," she said. "He's loved, *truly* loved by my Aunt Susie and Uncle Brian. And he has a good life. Just look at the life Jill and Andrew will give those twins. Those babies will be cherished and loved every minute of their lives. I knew my baby would have that when I decided I wasn't the one who should raise him."

"Then, you did the right thing, Pru. And nobody has the right to tell you otherwise."

"Do you really think I did the right thing? I mean, not because I think it's right. I mean, do *you* think it was right?" she asked.

"Yes, I really do."

She lay in his arms, no longer crying, and he held her, feeling her chest rise and fall with each breath until he felt her breaths even out. She fell asleep there, and he held her for a long time, knowing she needed to sleep. She needed to recharge if they were going to deal with this.

Gabe thought about the times he'd seen pictures of her with

her cousin, Matthew. She was close to him. That much was clear. He wondered if the boy knew. Maybe he didn't even know he was adopted. If he did, had he ever suspected PJ was his birth mother?

Gabe would call Chad as soon as she woke up and get him started trying to track down whoever had her journal, and held this twisted grudge against Pru for her decision to put the baby up for adoption. Because lying here with her in his arms, Gabe realized, he was through trying to resist PJ, through trying to convince himself this wasn't the right time for whatever was happening between them.

Yes. It might be the very worst possible time for her to start a relationship, but he didn't care. She'd been alone long enough. And, he had a feeling she'd punished herself long enough for the decisions she'd made as a fifteen-year-old. It was time PJ allowed herself to be happy. And he'd be damned if he wasn't going to be a part of that.

CHAPTER 12

It took Gabe a while to convince PJ that getting Chad involved in the search for the person who had her journal was a safe move. She wouldn't talk to the police, and he didn't blame her. If they went to the police, someone, somewhere along the way would leak the story to the press. If they got the police involved, too many people along the chain of command could slip up, and the information could find its way to the wrong set of ears.

Officers working the case might have every intention of maintaining her privacy.... But that wouldn't stop the guy who delivers the mail, or someone else, from overhearing details of the case and calling his girlfriend to tell her he'd seen PJ Cantrell at the police station—and so on and so on. That wasn't the way to go.

Besides, Chad didn't need to follow any procedures or obtain any warrants, so he'd have more freedom to go after this guy.

Of course, he hadn't told PJ he'd already involved Chad. And, he didn't plan to. He'd just delete the software from his phone, and not let on that he knew about the texts before she showed him any of them.

When he finally convinced her it was safe to involve Chad

and one of his tech staff, Samantha, they headed out to walk to Chad's house.

Gabe took PJ's hand as they started up the beach.

"I'm really glad you came with me this week, Pru," he said and was rewarded with that bright easy smile she'd had since she woke up from her impromptu nap this afternoon.

She looked happier than he'd seen her look all week, despite the fact that she still had the weight of the missing journal and Jimmy Mondo's threats on her shoulders.

"Pru, why didn't your parents report Jimmy all those years ago?" he asked but squeezed her hand gently to soften the question.

She blew out a burst of air before answering. "I think they knew it would have crushed me to have this made public." She looked up at him, and suddenly she looked a lot younger than twenty-nine. "I really thought he loved me. It was stupid, but I believed I was really special. To have the world know I had been so foolish...." She shook her head before she continued.

"But, there was also the baby. Jimmy had demanded I get an abortion. I didn't want that. In the end, my family decided it would be better to break all ties with Jimmy. My parents told him they wouldn't report him if he let me out of my contract without any penalties. He never asked about the baby, and we never told him. I didn't fill in any name for the father on the birth certificate. It was probably the wrong thing to do, but I just didn't want him having anything to do with Matthew. I didn't want Jimmy to be able to touch him, to taint his world in any way. Although, looking back, I suppose we could have gotten his signature on the adoption papers by promising not to press charges against him."

"You didn't want him to know you hadn't aborted the baby, though," he said. Under the circumstances, he couldn't blame her.

"Yeah. I just didn't want him anywhere near the baby, you

know? Not after the way...." She didn't finish her thought, but she didn't have to. He got it.

He stopped them at the gate to Chad's backyard and pulled her to him, wrapping her up in his arms. She tilted her head up at him and smiled that smile again, and it cut right through him.

Gabe leaned in and brushed her lips softly at first, then harder. The kiss took on a life of its own. She wrapped her arms around him and he loved the feel of that, the feel of her trusting him, touching him, kissing him back with everything she had.

God, he wanted her more than he'd ever wanted any woman. He almost laughed. *Who was he kidding?* No other woman had come remotely close to the pull she had on him, the intensity of what he felt when he was with her. He broke away and looked at her.

He needed to keep himself together long enough to get Chad and Samantha—Chad's computer guru—on the case and give them the info they needed. Then, he could take PJ home and make love to her. They had three more days until she had to go back on tour. He planned to spend as much of that time exploring her mind and body as he could.

"Ready for this?" he asked but her eyes were glassy.

"Huh?" she asked, drawing a laugh from him.

"Ready to go see Chad and Sam?" he asked again.

"Oh! Um, yes," she said, and he laughed even more at the adorable blush creeping into her cheeks. She was sexy as hell when she was flustered. And, he wanted to see just how much more flustered he could make her. But, that would be later.

For now, he tugged her up onto the lawn, and they cut across Chad's backyard until they came to the stone wall that surrounded the house. They rang the bell and a little buzzer sounded.

The mechanical sound of the gate clicking free told Gabe Chad had unlocked it remotely. They walked through and found him waiting on the back patio for them.

"Thanks, Chad," Gabe said as they approached.

"You guys need to come see this," Chad said, skipping any greeting. The grim look on his face sent cold rushing through Gabe again. They followed Chad into the living room where Samantha was set up with a laptop in front of her.

The television was playing and a newscaster was talking about Jimmy Mondo.

"He died in a hospital in Los Angeles about an hour ago," Chad said quietly, and Gabe heard PJ's gasp beside him. He put his arm around her and drew her in closer as Chad continued.

"It was a car accident. They're saying it may have been alcohol related. Apparently he was seen at several clubs last night. There are conflicting accounts, so the cause of the accident isn't clear yet. Some people swear he was sober when they saw him, but others say he was completely wasted."

The small floating box behind the newscaster alternated between showing a headshot of Jimmy Mondo smiling his greasy smile at the camera, and showing a wrecked car in flames on the side of a highway somewhere.

PJ's face showed the horror she was feeling as she gaped at the screen.

Gabe wanted to draw her away.

"Check your phone, PJ," Gabe said, wondering if her black-mailer had something to do with this.

PJ was pale as she drew it out of her pocket. "I turned it off," she said. Her hands shook as she held the top button down and the phone booted to life, chiming seconds later to indicate a text was waiting.

Gabe watched as her face crumpled, and he caught her in his arms when she likely would have fallen to the floor. He scooped her up and brought her to the couch. Samantha hovered in the background—always more comfortable with computers than people—but Chad came and sat near them.

Gabe took the phone from PJ and read the text before passing it to Chad. Chad slipped away to where Sam sat with her computer and the two of them bent their heads over the screen murmuring quietly as they worked. The words of the most recent text echoed in his head.

Jimmy paid. Are you ready to pay, Pretty Pru?

No way in hell he would let PJ go back out on tour now. At least, not without going with her.

Gabe pulled his cell phone out of his pocket, and sent a quick text to his assistant so he could arrange coverage for all his meetings, and move dates of anything that couldn't be covered by someone else.

He cleared two weeks and he'd clear more if he needed to.

His next text was to Jesse's fiancé, Zach Harris, who owned a private security company. When he'd met PJ at Jack's party, he hadn't batted an eye when PJ was introduced. Zach and his company were very used to handling high-profile clientele and doing so discreetly and effectively.

Do you have any of your people available for personal security for PJ for the foreseeable future? She's been getting threats. I'll be with her, but I'd like additional security if you have anyone. I don't trust her security staff. They really aren't even off the suspect list themselves yet, so I need backup for her.

The response came back almost instantly.

I can send two of my people tomorrow morning. I can come over myself if you need someone before then.

Gabe texted back. *Tomorrow's fine. I really don't think anyone knows where she is right now. Thanks.*

He brushed her temple with his mouth. "You okay, Pru?" he asked, and she nodded before looking up at him.

"I guess I haven't been taking this seriously enough. Do you...?" She swallowed and licked her lips before she continued. "Do you really think he killed Jimmy?"

Gabe could see her blinking her eyes and knew she was close to crying. She was shaken more than she wanted to admit. That was Pru—always trying to be tough, not letting people see what she was really feeling or how hard things really were.

He'd seen her do the same thing on tour. She had this crazy hard work ethic, and truly believed she'd been given a gift in her stardom. She believed she owed her fans for the opportunity they'd given her...the life they'd given her. And, he knew, she'd work forever to try to pay them back for that.

Now that he knew what had really happened thirteen years ago, he had a feeling she felt the same way about her parents. As if they'd given her a second shot at a career she'd almost thrown away with her alcohol abuse.

Her parents had helped give her child a chance at a life that was more than she would have been able to give the baby as a fifteen-year-old. Gabe looked her in the eye, knowing her tough-girl act was held together by a very thin strand at the moment.

"There's a possibility Jimmy just got drunk and stupid and crashed his car on his own. It's not like the man isn't known to drink. But—whether this guy's just taking credit for an accident or really had something to do with it—I don't want to take any chances. I cleared my schedule for a while so I can go with you for your next few tour stops, and I've got Zach sending extra security over tomorrow."

Chad approached and sat on the sofa across from them.

"What have you got, Chad?" Gabe asked.

"The blackmailer is using burn phones to send his texts. So far, he's used three different phones. With some carriers, we can get more than just the number. With other carriers, information like texts and calls is never recorded. So, if the person paid in cash for the phone, and paid cash for a phone card to charge up the phone, there's no way to trace it. That's what we've got here. Your guy knows how to stay anonymous."

"There's nothing you can do to trace it? Even if we're monitoring her phone when a text comes in?" Gabe asked.

Chad shook his head, his mouth set in a tight line. "Sorry.

There's no way to trace it. Even if we got the police involved, they wouldn't be able to get the information either. It simply isn't there to get, and I think your guy knows that."

Chad turned to PJ, who sat tense and anxious next to Gabe. "Based on what Gabe's told me, it's safe for us to assume this was someone close to you, correct?"

Gabe could feel the intake of breath as PJ seemed to brace herself for the conversation. He couldn't blame her. The idea that this was someone close to her killed him. It had to be tearing her apart inside, too.

"Right," she said, quietly. "No one knows I keep that journal. I'm careful only to get it out when I'm alone in my room, and I put it back each time I finish. I never write in it around anyone; even my parents didn't know it was there."

Chad's face creased in thought.

"What?" Gabe asked, knowing Chad had a theory.

"You don't travel in a typical bus like other singers? You only use Gabe's hotels?" When PJ nodded, Chad continued. "Who preps your room for you when you arrive at a new hotel? Does someone go in ahead of you, other than the hotel staff, that is?"

"Usually either Lydia or Ellis. Sometimes Debra if she's with us, but she doesn't travel with us very often. One of my body-guards accompanies hotel staff when they take my luggage up to the hotel room. Ellis or Lydia often have things to drop off for me, or they may be in there laying out clothes for interviews, shows, that kind of thing." PJ blushed a stark red.

"I guess it sounds like I'm a spoiled princess, but I usually have to go over to the venue and do a sound check or talk to the guys in my band. They travel in a bus and not with us. They prefer that."

"Why don't you travel by bus too?" Chad asked, and Gabe saw PJ flush again.

"I don't—" She paused and glanced at Gabe. "It's just that it reminds me of what it was like when I first started my career...of what happened with Jimmy."

Gabe had filled Chad in on the whole story before they'd come over, everything from the baby to Jimmy's agreement to let her out of her contract, to his recent angry text messages.

Gabe squeezed PJ's hand and rubbed his thumb over hers where their hands were joined.

"PJ, did you leave your luggage at the hotel with Lydia and Ellis, or do you have it here with you?" Chad asked.

"Most of it is with the team. I only brought a small bag with me," she answered. "Why?"

"The way I figure it, someone had to have found out about the journal. If you had a bus you used regularly, I'd check it for peep-holes of some sort in your section. Some way someone could spy on you." PJ's intake of breath was sharp and audible. She shook her head. "No one, no.... Not on my team."

This last part was weak. They all knew it had to be someone on her team, but it sounded as if she wasn't ready to face that possibility.

"I'd like to check your luggage to see if anyone's tampered with it or planted cameras in your belongings. That's really the only way someone could have seen you write in your journal and known where to look for it. Where are Debra and the rest of your team now?" Chad asked.

"Debra went on to Denver. She's in the Towers there, getting ready for the next show. She plans to stay with us for a few stops until this all dies down, then she'll go back to her office. I think the rest of the team was given a few days off. They'll meet us in Denver for the show. They should arrive tomorrow."

"Give me a minute," Chad said and crossed back over to speak to Sam. They could hear him instructing her to send two of his people to Denver to screen all of PJ's luggage. He also sent someone to the hotel in New York where she'd been when all this blew up to search the hotel suite there for any evidence that someone had been spying on her.

PJ sank forward, her head in her hands, and Gabe rubbed her back. He wanted to say something, anything, that could make this better for her, but he knew there wasn't anything to say.

Whoever this was, would prove to be a huge and very personal betrayal by someone she loved very much – or at the very least, trusted. Chad returned, sitting down across from them once again.

Before he had a chance to speak, Samantha stood and came over to them, holding her laptop.

"Chad, you need to see this."

Gabe leaned in. "What is it, Samantha?"

Chad was watching something on the screen intently. Samantha looked up at Gabe and explained.

"I've been looking at footage from security cameras and sightings posted on social media of PJ coming and going from her venues and from the hotels."

Gabe's eyes widened. "That's a lot of footage."

Sam waved a hand. "There are algorithms involved. And I told the computer to look for a few people, so it's not really me doing the looking."

Gabe knew Sam was a genius with computers. She had a game out that had been some kind of instahit when it released the year before. And he knew she'd worked for the FBI.

But he'd never seen her in action like this. He was glad she was here helping them.

"What did you find?" Pru asked.

Chad turned the screen toward them and played a clip. It was grainy like it had come from a security camera, and a cheap one at that. He saw PJ's limo pull up to his hotel in New York City.

"That's after a show two months ago," Pru said.

"Yeah, New York," Sam said. She pointed to a corner of the screen. "Watch here."

Pru went into the hotel with her security by her side. Seconds later, a woman stepped out from the shadow of the building and followed Pru into the building.

A gasp had Gabe looking at Pru. She was staring at the video.

"That's Erika Wilde."

Gabe knew the name, but couldn't place it.

Pru filled him in. "She's Kurt's girlfriend. The one he left me for."

"Do you think it's a coincidence she's at the hotel?" Pru asked.

Chad shook his head. "Sam found another video of her in the hotel lobby the following day when you were leaving for the venue you were playing that weekend."

"I cross checked Kurt's band's schedule with your tour and there are two more times you guys were in the same city near the same time. I've got the computer looking for videos from those cities now."

"You guys can go back to your house, Gabe. Sam and I will be running full background checks on your team, the band, your bodyguards—anyone who could be behind this, PJ. We'll keep going on the Erika lead also. We'll come by to talk about the results tomorrow. You have security arriving in the morning, Gabe?"

"Yes, Zach's sending two of his people over at daybreak. We'll keep them at the house with us, and then take them with us when we go on the road."

Gabe could feel PJ's eyes on him. He hadn't exactly told her he planned to go on her tour with her and stay on the tour for as long as she needed.

"All right. Sam and I will be over in the morning, but I'll call if we find anything major in the meantime. Let me know if you hear from this guy again."

Gabe nodded and pulled PJ up to her feet, then guided her to the back door. She seemed a bit shell-shocked as they walked back down the beach.

CHAPTER 13

*P*J felt numb as they walked up through Gabe's backyard. He entered the code to the back gate and held it open for her, then ensured that it clicked shut behind them before they continued up to the patio.

When her phone chimed, she pulled it out of her pocket, tense but comforted when she felt Gabe's strong hand on her back. She didn't mind at all that he looked over her shoulder, and she angled the phone toward him to allow him to see. Aunt Susie and Uncle Brian had sent a text.

Call when you can.

She hit the button to make the call and put the phone to her ear. Brian picked up almost immediately.

"What is it?" PJ asked. "Is Matthew all right?"

"Yes, PJ. But, we wanted to let you know," he paused, and she felt a jagged pain in her gut, dreading what was coming. *Had her blackmailer found Matthew? Had he contacted them?*

Brian continued. "We told Matthew about you. We told him you're his birth mother."

PJ felt hollow and then felt Gabe's arm around her, all but holding her up. Her head was reeling. "I always thought.... Well, I always just assumed...."

Matthew had known for years that he was adopted, but they hadn't told him PJ was his birth mother until now. She thought she'd be a part of that conversation when the time came.

"I'm sorry, PJ," Brian's voice softened. "We just felt we needed to tell him before he found out some other way. We didn't want to wait and then have him see something on the news."

She squared her shoulders. "Yeah.... No, I get it. That's fine, Brian. I understand. How did he take it? Can I talk to him?"

There was hesitation in his voice when he answered. "I'm sorry, Peej, honey. He's upstairs. He doesn't want to talk right now. I think he's still processing it."

PJ broke down when she heard that. Tears ran down her cheeks as Gabe's arms came around her and held her tight. She tried to talk, tried to ask if Brian thought Matthew would be all right, but she couldn't.

In her head, all she could do was berate herself for crying like this. Matthew was the important one. Only his feelings mattered here.

But somehow, knowing he knew the truth about where he'd come from and might choose never to speak to her again...well, it brought back all of the memories of having to turn over her tiny, incredible, precious baby the day he was born.

For months after she gave him up, her arms felt hollow, like she should be holding him but wasn't.

Even though she had given him to people she knew in her heart, with all her heart, would care for him and love him as if he were their own, she'd still felt the agony of letting someone else raise her child.

Now, she could be losing Matthew all over again.

She heard Brian soothing her. "It'll be okay, PJ. Matthew just needs time, but he loves you. And, he knows we're all there for him. He'll come around."

PJ felt Gabe take the phone from her hand. "Brian, she'll call you back."

PJ would like to say she was strong, that she brushed away the tears and collected herself and all was good and well in the world....

It wasn't. And she didn't. Gabe lifted her and she let him. She rested her head against his chest and sobbed as he carried her to the house and into her room.

Gabe sat on the edge of her bed, letting her settle into his lap.

PJ couldn't believe she'd let him see her fall apart like this. She was a grown woman, for heaven's sake. But, she also hadn't had any warning, had no idea she was about to hear what she had. *What if Matthew didn't ever want to speak with her? What if he didn't want her in his life? What if she couldn't be a part of his life? Couldn't see him growing up?*

Part of her knew it had been better for him to find out this way than to discover it when or if it leaked to the media, but that didn't lessen the pain.

It took a long time for her tears to stop and when they did, she was spent. Beyond spent.

Gabe seemed to read her mind. He laid her on her bed and then pulled the covers back to tuck her in. As she closed her eyes, the last thing she was aware of was the sense of security, the feeling of unquestionable support, as Gabe stretched out and lay down next to her, one arm slung over her as he pulled her close.

CHAPTER 14

$\mathcal{G}$abe watched PJ's breath as it evened out. She had fallen asleep in minutes, if not seconds. Her face relaxed in sleep as the grief fell away.

He couldn't even begin to imagine what she was feeling, but he hated seeing her so torn apart. She had been ripped to shreds by all this, and he hated not being able to do anything to fix it.

He wanted to stay next to her for as long as she needed him, but he heard the faint buzz of the front gate alert from the kitchen, and didn't want to risk it buzzing again. If the dark circles under her eyes were any indication, PJ needed to rest for a long time.

Gabe went to the kitchen and pressed the intercom to the front gate. "Yes?" he said into the speaker.

"Courier delivery for Gabe Sawyer."

"What company are you with?"

The courier didn't hesitate at the question. "Long and Short Overnight Service, sir."

"Thank you. Come on up." Gabe hit the button to open the gate and walked out to the front door to meet the courier at the top of the drive. His secretary always used the same company when she had to send something to him that couldn't be done by fax or DocuSign.

Gabe still worked with a few people in the industry who were old school and didn't trust the security of online document signing services. Although Gabe found that ridiculous, and more than once had been tempted to break ties because of the inconvenience, they'd been good companies to work with in all other ways, so he'd persevered.

Relationships were crucial to Gabe's success. Burning bridges over the use of a courier to deliver a few things here and there didn't seem worth the trade-off in the end.

The courier handed him a letter-sized envelope and waited for him to sign a paper before getting back in his van and leaving the way he'd come. Gabe waited until the gate closed behind the courier's car and returned to the kitchen, tossing the envelope on the kitchen counter before grabbing a soda from the fridge.

Gabe chugged half the can before turning to the envelope and tearing it open. Instead of a contract, the stack of papers that slid out turned his blood hot and cold all at once.

Shit.

The pages were filled with nothing but the words, 'It's almost time, Pretty Pru' over and over again. There must have been twenty or thirty pages with nothing but the same message. And right on top of the stack was a photo. A small, worn, wallet-sized photo of a baby. Gabe knew without asking Pru who the baby was. It was Matthew. Gabe was sure of it.

Gabe went to look in on PJ, and saw she was still sleeping in the other room. He dialed Zach's phone and was relieved when Zach picked up right away.

"Zach, it's Gabe. He knows she's here. He knows she's with me." He quickly explained about the courier delivery, especially the part where the blackmailer or stalker or whatever the hell you call a guy who hasn't actually made a demand for money, had used the same courier service that Gabe's secretary always used.

"On my way," Zach said before hanging up and Gabe knew he'd be there in half an hour, or less. That's the way his friends in Connecticut were. It was the reason he had bought the house here, why he planned to settle here someday—probably sooner rather than later.

After the accident that killed his dad and sister, he didn't have much family left. Only his mom and she didn't recognize him most of the time now. That made the connections he'd found in the people around him all the more important.

There wasn't a damn thing they all wouldn't do for each other. No questions asked. Anytime. Here he had the kind of friendships he never imagined.

His next call was to Chad to let him know about the photo. Gabe had a feeling the picture belonged to PJ. He'd ask her about it as soon as she woke up, but in the meantime, he wanted to see what Chad had found.

"Let me know as soon as you talk to PJ about the picture. We need to know if it's hers—and if it is, where she kept it. This asshole's close to her," Chad said, and Gabe could tell from his voice Chad was taking this personally.... If Gabe cared for PJ, then Chad would, too. It was that simple with his friends.

"Listen, Gabe," Chad went on. "Did you know Ellis White was adopted? His family adopted him when he was twelve, after he was passed around to a lot of different foster homes. Apparently, his biological mother left him at a mall when he was eight years old."

"Pru never mentioned that. I wonder if she knows. I remember her saying Ellis and Lydia are siblings, and she didn't always like the way Lydia treated Ellis. I don't remember her mentioning adoption, though."

"Whoever's doing this sounds angry, Gabe. Angry and vindictive. And, they've had a lot of access to PJ," Chad said.

"You think it might be Ellis?" Gabe asked, knowing the answer, but dreading the idea of going to Pru with that theory. It would tear her up to think one of her team could be behind this.

Gabe spun at the sound of Pru's small voice behind him. "It's not Ellis."

She shook her head at Gabe, one hand over her stomach as if he'd just physically cut into her with his accusation. "It's not Ellis. Our families have been friends for years. And you don't know Ellis like I do. He's kind and gentle. There's no way he'd do something like this."

"I'll call you back," Gabe said, and set his phone on the counter before crossing to Pru. He pulled her in close for a hug, her small frame fitting snugly against him.

She pulled back, but not as if to pull away. She leaned back and looked up at him. "It's *not* Ellis," she repeated.

"I want to believe that too, Pru," he said, "but we need to look at the facts and not dismiss anyone without considering everything carefully. Whoever is doing this is close to you. It's most likely going to be someone you trust. It may even be someone you love. But, it's almost certainly someone close, Pru."

She bowed her head a minute and took a deep breath, before lacing her hand behind Gabe's neck and pulling him down into a heated kiss that threw Gabe completely off balance and curdled his brains.

On some level, he knew it was wrong. Everything in him was screaming to stop, to not allow her to do this when she was in such emotional turmoil. But, his body utterly overrode anything his head knew.

He was instantly hard as a rock, his cock pressing against his pants for release as his hands wrapped around her waist, lifting her to the counter.

He knew she was probably just trying to forget, just trying to slip away from reality for a short time before her world came crashing down, but he couldn't bring himself to stop her.

He felt her tremble as his mouth devoured her, her moans driving his mouth down her jaw to the small spot behind her neck that seemed to cause her body to bow, arching into him. He'd never felt a hotter, faster burn in his body than the fire Pru set loose in him.

He pulled open the sheer white blouse that had been tempting him for hours, exposing her incredibly perfect breasts. They weren't large by any means, but to him, they were everything he'd ever wanted. One hand traced the outer edge of her breast softly, almost reverently, as he dipped his head to suck the nipple on her other breast, drinking her in.

She rewarded him with a quick intake of breath as her nipples pearled and a moan began deep in her throat.

PJ's head reeled as Gabe assaulted her with more feeling, more sensation than she'd ever felt. She had wanted to forget, to think of something other than fear and betrayal and loss for just a short time. He was giving her that and so much more.

She was wet and swollen and ready for him when he slipped his hand beneath her skirt and roughly pulled her panties to the side, sinking his fingers into her. Her whole body tightened around him as his thumb circled her clit, and she was lost in an instant. Utterly lost to the feeling of him touching her, of his mouth on her breasts, of all of him devouring her with such complete--

A small part of her heard the buzzer of the front gate, but Gabe's mouth sucked hard on her nipple at the same time that he added just slightly more pressure with his thumb...at the same time that he found the precise spot inside her and set off a cascading orgasm, drenching her in pleasure she'd never felt before.

She was weak and spinning when he pulled back and lowered her dress. His voice was gravelly and low when he spoke.

"Go to my bedroom," he said, slipping her off the counter. "If I don't let Zach in soon, he's going to let himself in."

It took PJ a minute to grasp what he'd said as he gave her a gentle push toward his bedroom door. *Zach. Zach was coming over.* "I'll be there in a minute, Pru."

Why was Zach coming here?

PJ didn't know why Gabe had called Zach here. Worse, she didn't know what Gabe thought about what they'd just done. She could feel the heat burning her cheeks as she remembered the way she'd cried out his name as she'd orgasmed in his arms moments before. One minute they'd been talking and the next, she'd jumped on him. And, he'd brought her to orgasm in seconds flat.

Oh, god. He must think she was such a whore. In the last few days, he'd learned more than she'd ever wanted him to about her sex life with Kurt Tolleson, and he'd heard about her losing her virginity to a man who was twenty years her senior.

And now, she'd spread her legs for him and come in an astonishingly fast fashion for him. Would he think she was a complete slut? It was almost laughable, given her lack of experience with men, but she still felt embarrassed at how forward she'd been.

As she entered his room, she wanted to be anywhere but there. She wanted to run and hide, to pack her bags and hide out where no one could find her. To be alone again.

But even as she thought it, she knew she was tired of being alone, of only having her parents and the closest members of her team as friends. There hadn't really been anyone else in a long time.

Her high school friends had all gone on to lead such different lives than the one she'd led. They had tried to stay close to her, but honestly, after her spiral with alcohol and the baby and the fight to get herself on track, she'd felt alienated and removed from them. Not *by* them.

It was something internal. Something she felt had created a wall between her and her friends. It was as though they were no longer able to connect.

She had no friends who would do what Jill and Andrew's friends had done: rally around when she needed them. Well, except for Gabe. He had rallied for her the second he found out she was in trouble. He'd been there for her, and he was still here for her.

And then it dawned on PJ. that Gabe had seemed to be expecting Zach, even though Gabe had told Zach earlier they wouldn't need him to come tonight. Something had changed Gabe's mind about Zach coming to the house.

PJ stood and straightened her skirt, buttoned her shirt and pulled her hair up in a knot, then pushed the door to the room open. Both men were bent over the kitchen island looking at papers.

"What happened, Gabe?" she asked, but it came out more as an accusation. "What aren't you telling me?"

He tried a halfhearted 'it's nothing' kind of response, but she put her hands on her hips and waited him out.

He picked up the envelope and handed her the sheets of paper. "These came to me by courier while you were sleeping," he said as she read the sheaf of papers. *It's almost time, Pretty Pru. It's almost time, Pretty Pru. It's almost time, Pretty Pru.*

She looked up at Gabe and Zach. "He knows where I am."

Gabe's face was grave as he nodded. "Yes, he knows."

She looked at him and knew he wasn't telling her everything. "What are you hiding?"

"This came, too," he said quietly. She knew what it was the minute she saw it. Matthew's baby picture. The one she'd carried with her until it was lost a month ago. The photo of him the day he was born.

PJ didn't hesitate. She dropped the photo back on the counter as though it had bit her, and ran to her room and began haphazardly shoving her things into her bag. She needed to get to Matthew.

Gabe and Zach followed her. She felt Gabe's arms come around her, stilling her hands and stopping her frantic packing.

Zach came around in front of her. "PJ, I've got guys headed that way now. They'll have Matthew and his family on the road within the hour, and they'll get them to a safe place. Somewhere we can control."

Gabe kept talking to her, his breath warm and reassuring as her heart raced in her chest. "They'll get to them, Pru. I promise. We'll keep Matthew safe. I'll keep you both safe."

But PJ didn't care about her own safety anymore. In a heartbeat, she'd give herself to whoever it was that was doing all of this in exchange for Matthew's safety.

Her whole body was weak and shaking. She walked to the couch and sat, Gabe following. She let him, but as she sat and looked at him, she felt angry. Angry at how helpless and powerless this person made her feel. Angry at how she let this blackmailer make her hide, make her run and curl up in a ball.

She was done with that. She sat up and looked at Gabe.

"Show me the picture again," she said. She expected them to argue, but neither man did.

Zach sat across from them as she studied the picture. Matthew was only hours old in the picture. Looking at the photo, no one would be able to make out who was holding him, but she knew it was one of a handful of times she'd held him when he was that young. After she left the hospital, she hadn't let herself visit him for almost two years.

She had known she wouldn't be able to handle the pain of seeing him and having to say good-bye afterwards. When he was two, it was harder than she'd expected, but by then he'd truly been Brian and Susan's baby. She was able to see him in that light instead of as the son she'd given up.

"This was in my wallet until about a month ago," she said. "I lost it when we were in Indianapolis at the Kulsich Music Center. I had it out in my dressing room, and then I forgot to put it back when I closed up my purse before the show. I just figured one of the team tossed it by mistake when they were clearing my dressing room in a rush to move on. I planned to get another copy of it when I saw Brian and Sue again. They have a few pictures from that day."

Zach picked up his phone and sent a text. "Indianapolis was one of the cities where Kurt's band was there a day after yours. I'll see if Samantha found any footage showing Erika hanging around."

PJ looked up. "She texted me a lot after Kurt left me for her. She was obsessed, always telling me I had to stay away from him. I changed my phone number and the messages stopped."

She lifted the picture again and stared at the image of Matthew, so small and vulnerable. He was still vulnerable, even though he was older now.

Zach spoke up as Gabe rubbed her back, the hand that had set her on fire only a short while before now soothing her— adding his strength to hers.

"PJ, I don't think this picture means the person actually knows who Matthew is or where he is. If they had identified him and his family, they would have sent a current picture of him. We'll take precautions as though he's in danger to be on the safe side, but I think this is just your blackmailer's way of trying to get to you."

Gabe nodded. "Everything he's done shows he's angry with *you*, Pru, not with Matthew."

"Okay, but don't blackmailers usually ask for something? Money? This guy still hasn't made any actual demands," she said, taking a deep breath. "What did Chad find in the background checks of my team?"

Her team had all been vetted heavily when they applied to work for her, so she couldn't imagine finding anything she didn't already know about.

"So far the biggest red flag is Ellis's background. Did you know he's adopted?"

"Yes. Our parents were friends when we were little, although both Lydia and he were younger than me. He doesn't talk about it, and neither does his sister, Lydia. He was adopted by her parents when he was about twelve, I believe. It was awful, really. Lydia's dad died in a car accident shortly after Ellis was adopted. He only had the chance to have a father for a few months, I think. As far as I know, he has no contact with his biological family."

"Do you know anything about his background before he came to her family?" Gabe asked.

"A little. He was in foster homes a lot. And his mom had left him in the mall before that. You wouldn't know it, though. He's so sweet."

"How did they come to work for you?" Gabe asked.

"My mom thought of Lydia when I needed a tour manager several years ago. She'd been working in project management, I think. My mom still talks to her mom and she mentioned Lydia was looking for something new. She was perfect for the job. She runs everything and is on top of every detail. Ellis came to work for me about six months ago. She got him the interview and I was happy to hire him."

Zach spoke. "Chad's sending guys down to meet with your team, interview them and search your luggage. Whoever did this had to find your journal somehow. They had to have seen you or heard you at times you thought you were alone."

PJ flinched. The idea of someone spying on her made her very uncomfortable, as was the idea that Chad's people would have to put her team through this interrogation and scrutiny to find answers.

She couldn't help but think her team would feel they were being accused of something, not just being interviewed. She worried about how Ellis, in particular, would take that. She could picture how hurt he'd look, and the sense of betrayal that would show clearly on his gentle face.

"Chad also ran checks on your background singers and your band. A couple of little things popped here and there. A few with some minor criminal backgrounds. Jaqueline has lost several babies, so he's looking a little harder at her."

PJ flinched again. She hadn't known Jackie had lost any babies, and that invasion of the guitarist's privacy bit into her. What an awful thing to go through, but to have that bit of your life on record somewhere, a record that an investigator could find, made it all the worse. And, how would Jackie feel when the investigators raised that?

"I can't even call them and let them know Chad's people are coming, can I?" she asked, knowing they'd say no.

"No," said Zach, but then he surprised her. "We can arrange for you to talk to them as soon as the investigators get there. We'll get everyone into a conference room while we search luggage, the tour bus, everything. You can talk to them by phone and let them know a little about what's going on. It's not much, but it's the best we can do, PJ." Zach's phone buzzed. He glanced at it before looking back up at her.

"My guys have Matthew and his parents. They're safe."

Her heart felt like it would collapse inside her chest with relief when she heard those words. From the moment she'd decided to give birth to him when she was fifteen years old, that's all she'd ever wanted for Matthew. For him to be safe and loved.

Gabe stood and held out his hand to her. "Let's go to bed, Pru."

She stood and turned toward her room, but he tugged her

hand and pulled her toward his, bringing a hot flush to her cheeks.

Zach called out a good night from his place on the couch, and she wondered if he thought anything of the fact that Gabe was leading her to his bedroom.

Probably not. It's not like they lived in the eighteenth century. But still, the idea of Zach knowing she'd be sleeping in Gabe's bed was embarrassing. And yet, she wanted Gabe to hold her.

She still felt raw from having so easily slipped into a sexual relationship with Gabe, and they hadn't had a chance to talk about what had happened earlier. She had no idea what he was thinking or what he expected from her. Tonight or in the future. What would Gabe want from her? Was this a quick screw because he found out how easy she was? How she'd spread her legs so readily at fifteen?

Would he want to continue this beyond the end of the week? Or was she just another one of the stars she always saw on his arm at fundraisers? That thought bothered her. A lot. She wanted to be special to him. Just like she'd wanted to be special to Jimmy Mondo so many years ago.

She'd thought sex brought intimacy, but it didn't mean that at all. She had learned that lesson early, and she'd learned it well. And she'd remembered it until, apparently, this afternoon with Gabe. She'd forgotten everything she'd ever learned the moment his mouth had touched her.

That needed to stop.

Gabe shut the door behind them, and PJ was suddenly very aware of how alone they were, how close he stood.

"We can't do this," she said hurriedly, before she chickened out. "We can't sleep together."

His dark eyes studied her, but he didn't argue. "Sleep together or make love?"

Her heart leapt at his description of it as love not sex, but she knew better than to be fooled by sweet words. She cleared her throat to answer, but he moved before she could get anything out. He just turned and walked to his dresser on the other side of the room.

As she watched, he undid the button fly on his jeans in what seemed like one all-too-smooth move. He stripped down to his boxers and tossed his jeans over the arm of a wing-backed chair, then drew low-slung sweatpants up over his lean hips. He turned and watched her, those heated eyes never leaving hers, as he pulled his shirt over his head and replaced it with a T-shirt. He watched her as he reached back in the dresser and pulled out another pair of sweatpants and a T-shirt and crossed the room to where she stood, frozen, her heart pounding.

He didn't say a word as he placed the clothes in her hands, then pushed her toward the door of the bathroom and shut it behind her.

Well, that answers that question.

Apparently, tonight they were only going to sleep together – literally. And, it seemed that he was okay with that.

PJ frowned. He'd been easily convinced. Too easily and she wasn't sure she was okay with that, though that was what she'd asked for only moments before. No, not asked for. She'd demanded.

She quickly changed into the clothes he'd given her, laughing as she rolled the sweatpants up several times around the waistband. Nope. They still swam on her and slipped down when she moved. She took off the sweatpants and checked the length of his T-shirt. The hem fell to her thighs, and covered up more than he'd already seen when she'd been out by the pool in her bathing suit earlier in the day. It would do.

He'd laid out a new toothbrush and toothpaste on the counter and wondered when he'd done that. Exactly when had he come up with this plan for her to move into his room, she wondered as she opened the package and then brushed.

PJ took a deep breath before exiting the bathroom, but still wasn't prepared for the sight of Gabe in his bed. He lay on his back, covers draped loosely over his lap, arms crossed behind his head. But, as his eyes met hers, she saw he was anything but relaxed. His whole body seemed coiled and tense, and his eyes were heated, seeming to burn through her as he took in her bare legs.

"You're supposed to be wearing sweatpants," he all but growled as his arms came down from behind his head.

"They were too big," she squeaked when he sat up in the bed.

"Christ, woman," he swore as he threw back the covers. He pulled her toward the bed. "Under," he ordered and waited as she climbed under the covers.

Gabe drew the covers up to her chin, then lay down next to her, his body on top of the covers, drawing a laugh from her.

"It's not funny," he said, his grumbling making her laugh harder.

He rolled her toward him, covered her with his body and took her mouth, his own hot and hard and utterly unyielding on hers. PJ let out a moan as her body responded instantly, despite the layers of covers and clothes between their bodies.

She was suddenly needy and wet, and completely unable to focus on anything other than finding a way through the covers and clothes that divided their bodies.

And, then Gabe was rolling her over again, spooning her, one arm draped over her body, the evidence of his arousal evident, even through the covers.

"There," he said, triumph dripping from his voice. "You try to sleep now."

PJ didn't laugh this time.

CHAPTER 15

*G*abe would have preferred to spend the morning in bed with PJ, but with the way things were heading, he knew that wouldn't happen. Zach's light knock on his door had woken him early, and he'd come out to find Chad was already at the house.

Yeah, the whole lying-in-bed-with-PJ-for-hours thing wasn't going to happen.

"Give me a minute, guys," he said as Chad and Zach fought over who got first dibs on the espresso machine.

Gabe grabbed PJ's overnight bag from her guest room and crossed back to his room so she'd have something to put on when she woke up. She was still out cold when he put the bag at the foot of the bed so she'd see it when she woke. Man, he'd give anything to crawl back in bed with her.

After they got this under control and took care of whoever was making her so stressed right now, he'd take her away for a while. Maybe they'd find an island without phones or faxes or fans or crazed blackmailing stalkers and hole up there for a month. Or six.

Assuming she'd go with him, he thought, as he shut the door behind him and went to join the other men in the kitchen. He still wasn't entirely sure where he stood with Pru. What if she only wanted friendship after this was over? Could he still give her that if that was all she wanted?

"What've you got, guys?" he asked as he took a sip from the espresso Zach had just set down on the counter. He swallowed with a wince. "Jeez. I'll make my own," he said and handed the cup back to Zach.

"We'll need to have PJ talk to her people on a conference call in the next hour or so," Chad said. "My people are in place and are going to begin searching. The plan is to bring everyone on her team and in her band into one suite and let them know they can either submit to a search or lose their jobs. We'll pitch it that we believe the perp may be hiding things among them, bugging the tour bus and luggage and things. We'll ask for their cooperation first, but if we have to, we'll make it clear their jobs are on the line, and refusing will give the police reason to look into them further if we bring the police into this."

"Christ," Gabe swore. "PJ's gonna freak. I don't know if she'll be able to repair the damage that will be done, conference call or not."

"What am I gonna freak over?" came Pru's worried voice behind them.

Gabe turned to find she'd kept his T-shirt on but had slipped jeans under them. The effect of her ruffled hair, the oversized tee and her bare feet had him taking a step closer to the kitchen counter to hide his painfully obvious erection. The men in the room with him might be happily involved with women they loved, but he found himself wanting to toss them out so they couldn't see his Pru like this.

Zach was the first to answer PJ's question, and he sugarcoated it more than Gabe would have felt comfortable doing, so he was relieved he'd been too tongue-tied to answer her – so he didn't have to lie.

"Chad's guys are getting ready to question your people, so we just need to get you on a conference call to soften the blow a bit."

"Soften the blow?" she asked, an eyebrow raised. Yeah, okay, she wasn't an idiot. She wasn't going to fall for the sugarcoated version.

Gabe cleared his throat. "They'll be making it clear that their jobs are dependent on cooperating to find out who's doing this to you." A lot less sugar in that version.

Though she kept her face blank, he knew that had to be a blow. With the exception of her bodyguards who had been brought on last year when her old security team retired, she had been with her bandmates and team for years. Gabe was sure it killed her to let Chad make that kind of a threat to people she cared about.

"We'll ask for cooperation first, PJ. We'll stress you're in danger and other people have been threatened, and we'll ask for their help. We'll only pull out the threat of their jobs if anyone really balks," Chad said.

"When can we get them on a call together?" she asked quietly, and Gabe admired the hell out of her as she steeled her spine and pulled herself together to face this. She wasn't falling apart anymore. Damn if he didn't love that about her. Her strength and resilience.

"Our guys are getting your people together now. We'll set up a call with you in a half hour," Chad said, then rubbed his forehead. "Listen, there's something else we found."

Gabe wanted to ask what now, but waited for Chad to say more instead.

"Sam's traced a few sales of pictures of you," he said to Pru, "back to one of your security guys." He raised his hand to Gabe's low growl. "Nothing like what you're thinking. Just a couple images of her getting ready to go on stage, that kind of thing. Still, not something he should be selling when he's supposed to be working for you."

"Which one?" Pru asked and Gabe couldn't help but think the arm she had wrapped over her stomach was a protective gesture, like she could ward off the blow. It seemed impossible for her to trust anyone in the world she lived in.

"Carl," Chad said, "though I have to wonder if your other guy knew about it. Seems like he'd have seen Carl snap those pictures. It might be worth hiring a whole new security team."

Pru nodded but she looked sick to her stomach. "Do you have a way to get in touch with Brian and Susie? I want to check on Matthew."

Chad pulled his phone out and keyed a button, then waited while the phone rang.

"Hey," Chad said into the phone, as Gabe went to PJ and kissed her on the temple, drawing her close to him with one arm. He was relieved when she sank against him, aligning her body with his. He'd been a little unsure of what she'd be like with him this morning.

Chad passed the phone to PJ a minute later, and she tugged Gabe by the arm over to the couch with her, obviously not caring if he heard the conversation. What a wuss ass he was for the wave of relief he felt at that.

"Hi Brian. Is Matthew up yet?" Pru asked. Gabe could hear the answer, "Yes, he's having breakfast," through the speaker phone.

"How's he doing today?" she asked and Gabe heard the tension in her voice, the desperation to have Matthew confirm that he still loved her, still wanted her in his life.

"He's better, Peej. He's coming to terms with it. We also talked, and we want to let you know it's okay if you have to tell your story yourself. If you have to tell the media who Matthew is. He's already used to getting attention because he's your cousin. He'll have the spotlight on him if the story comes out, but we'll be there for him, and the attention will die down quickly."

Gabe had already considered having Pru release her version

of the story herself before the guy coming after her did. Even so, they'd still need to find out who this was because they would remain a threat to Pru—but having the story released would take some of the stress out of the situation. It would also ensure no one ever held this over Pru's head again after this guy was caught.

"I'll think about it," PJ said and her eyes met Gabe's.

Oh, he was such an ass for being so damned happy she looked to him for support. Such an ass.

"Hang on, Peej," Brian said. "Matthew wants to talk to you."

Gabe heard a choked sob come from PJ, and he tightened his hold around her shoulders. Chad and Zach had slipped out to the patio, leaving only her and Gabe in the room, and he was glad she'd have privacy for this. Her hand landed on Gabe's chest where her fingers closed around his shirt, clutching him tight.

Gabe couldn't hear anything from the other end of the phone, but PJ must have heard something. "You there, Matthew?"

There was a small sound from the phone. It wasn't quite a grunt, but just a murmur that let them know Matthew was on the phone.

"Please don't tell me I've lost you again, Matthew. I don't want to lose you," PJ begged, and Gabe would give anything to make this better for her. To make her heart whole again.

"Dad said you were fifteen years old," came Matthew's quiet voice.

"Yes," PJ said and Gabe saw her close her eyes. "Almost sixteen when you were born." He didn't know whether she was praying for more or thankful for small gifts. He was praying for more. He wanted Matthew, who was much too young to have to be this mature, to find the strength to forgive Pru. The strength to let Pru remain a part of his life.

There was silence on the line for a long time as PJ and Gabe waited.

"I'm thirteen," Matthew said and Gabe held his breath. The

kid was doing the math. He was putting it together. He under-stood how young Pru was when she had him.

Pru waited.

"You coming home for my birthday, Aunt PJ?" Matthew finally asked, his voice cracking a bit as he spoke, and Gabe watched as Pru cried and nodded, trying to say yes into the phone, but not quite getting anything out.

An hour later, showered and dressed, they met with Chad and Zach in the kitchen and looked at all the information they had gathered to that point.

"So far, your blackmailer hasn't done anything that required him or her to leave the tour, other than possibly tampering with Jimmy Mondo's car or somehow setting Jimmy's accident in motion. And in reality, we still don't know for sure that's what happened. Jimmy's death could have been an accident," Chad said.

Zach cut in. "We've got a few friends on the police force in Los Angeles where the accident took place. We're waiting to hear if the car had been tampered with, and to get a tox screen back on Jimmy to see what was in his system."

Chad nodded. "So far, everything your guy's been doing has been from behind the scenes, hiding behind texts and messenger services. It's highly likely that this person's absence from your team would be noticed at any exact moment, and it would be easy to connect that absence with any attack on you here."

Chad pulled his cell phone out and read from the notes app on the screen. "Unfortunately, your entire team hasn't been together since you arrived here. Your tour bus was sent ahead to your next tour stop in Denver and the driver has been waiting at the Towers there. Your team and band met them there yesterday, but between then and now, Debra has gone back to her office, and Ellis and Lydia took two days off. Ellis said he was driving across the country, stopping at civil war monuments on the way. He met up with Lydia at the Towers in Denver late yesterday afternoon."

"So, it's possible he could have gone out to LA and tampered with Jimmy Mondo's car before meeting up with Lydia?" Gabe asked.

Chad nodded. "Exactly. But, the others are equally unaccounted for. Lydia supposedly stayed at the Towers in New York for two days before she went to Denver. But, since checkout is automated and there's no record of her using room service or anything, we'll need to get someone on the ground there to see if any of the staff remember seeing her. Gabe, can you take care of that for us?"

"Yep. I'm on it," Gabe said, sending a quick text to the general manager of the Towers New York asking him to send security footage from the hotel lobby and all other public areas for the day Jimmy was killed, and to see if any of the staff remembered seeing Lydia that day.

"There's also the band. They split up and went their separate ways. The driver of the tour bus continued on to Denver, and the various members of the band each went to stay with friends. We're working on getting in touch with the friends they saw, trying to confirm they were with them for the days we need to track," Zach said.

"So you think the reason this person hasn't actually come after me yet is because they can't slip away from the group unnoticed?" PJ asked.

Chad nodded. "I think so. They clearly know where you are. They know a lot about you, and about Gabe, it seems. Enough to know he owns this house—that not many people know about—and what courier Gabe's assistant uses to send things to him here. This person must be someone who moves around the Towers properties easily and unnoticed."

"Lydia and Ellis are often in the Towers offices talking to my staff about arrangements for PJ," Gabe said. "We let her security move around the hotel so they can check on things for her. I don't think the band would move around easily in the back areas."

Chad nodded, making notes before looking at PJ. "Who did you tell about your plan to stay with Gabe?"

"Only Debra and my parents should know where I am right now. I didn't tell the rest of the team, and I asked Debra not to share it with them," PJ answered.

"I think whoever this is wanted to scare you with Jimmy's death, but now, unless they can somehow arrange for everyone to split up again, it would be obvious who it was the minute someone comes after you. All we would need to do is look to see who's missing, and we'd know who to go after," Chad said.

PJ was quiet for a minute, and Gabe felt his gut clench. He knew what she was thinking before she voiced it a split second later. "I need to go back."

"No, Pru," he said quietly, but not at all softly. Her gaze cut to him quickly, but she looked away. She looked back to Chad and Zach, squaring her shoulders.

"No!" Gabe said, not even going for quiet this time.

"Let's head back," PJ said, completely ignoring him. Chad and Zach were silent, their eyes watching PJ and Gabe as Gabe came up behind her and turned her to face him.

"Are you crazy? You're just going to walk back there and let this guy do whatever he wants to you? Is this some kind of twisted punishment you feel the need to take on because you gave Matthew up? Because Matthew's forgiven you. He's happy and safe. He has everything you ever wanted for him. You don't need to do this."

PJ's eyes flashed, and she put her hands on her hips and squared off with him. "What would you have me do, Gabe? Hide out here with you forever? Give up my career? Leave my life because some sick, twisted asshole has it out for me?"

"It's a start," Gabe said, hearing how insane he sounded, hearing how idiotic that plan was. Of course she couldn't hide out forever. But, he wouldn't watch her walk back in and hand herself over to this guy.

He saw Chad and Zach slip out of the kitchen and knew they'd probably station themselves in the front of the house, or one in the back and one out front. Either way, they were giving him and PJ space—and he appreciated it.

He needed to find a way to talk some sense into her. To hell with talking. He didn't want to talk. He wanted to drag her off to his room and lock her in. And never let her out.

Realistic? Probably not, based on the way she was looking at him...like she'd draw and quarter him if he tried.

"Pru, please," he started. "Let's just find a better way to deal with this than sticking you out there as bait for this lunatic. Whoever he is, he's angry and resentful, and he didn't hesitate to kill Jimmy. If he gets to you––"

PJ knew Gabe wanted to take care of everything for her. He'd try to fix everything and make sure she never had to worry about anyone coming after her again. He'd find a way to get her journal back, to stop the person who was doing this to her. To take care of it all. And a big part of her really wanted to let him do that. Wanted it in a way she never had before, not even with Jimmy way back when.

But, the thing was, she was twenty-nine years old and so far, she hadn't had a whole lot of luck with men. At each and every turn, men had stabbed her in the back and walked away when she needed them. Jimmy hadn't batted an eye before telling her to get rid of 'the problem,' as he'd referred to the baby growing in her stomach when she was just fifteen.

And Kurt? Well, Kurt had walked away without a backward

glance. She'd been with other men here or there, but never risked her heart after that.

The only times she'd risked her heart, it had been trampled on.

And with Gabe, PJ was no idiot. She knew her heart was on the line in a way it had never been before. All of those foolish entries in her journal about her feelings for those other men.... They were nothing compared to what she already felt for Gabe.

And, that scared the crap out of her. She might want Gabe more than she'd ever wanted any other man, but she wasn't willing to take a chance on seeing where things might go with him.

What would happen when he got tired of her and walked away? That would do her in. It would finish her. So she did the only thing she could to protect her heart.

"I don't think you should come back with me, Gabe," PJ said, standing taller and looking him in the eye. She saw the pain in his eyes, his confusion.

"What? Why, Pru?" His voice was quiet and low, sending an unwanted chill up her spine. He stepped in even closer to her and she had to put a hand out to his chest to steady herself.

Contact. Big mistake. She drew her hand back quickly.

"I think I need to do this on my own for now. I need to deal with this myself."

His eyes went wide, and she could feel the intensity of his stare as she glanced away. "Look, Gabe, I...I haven't really done very well in the relationship department. It.... They don't tend to end very well for me. And, it's just.... It's not something I want to go through right now. I just need to deal with this – to focus on this stalker or blackmailer or whatever this person is. I just need to face this and stop running and deal with this...this—"

"Try 'killer.' Killer is the word you're looking for. This person killed Jimmy, and now he's flat out told you he's coming after you, and you're planning to run into his arms completely unprotected," Gabe said, anger rolling off him, palpable and more than a little intense.

She raised her chin. "Fine. *Killer*. But I'm not going back completely unprotected. I'll have Chad and Zach and their whole team with me. And, my own security guys," she finished.

"Who haven't actually been cleared by Chad and who've done a piss-poor job of protecting you so far. For all we know, it could be one of them," Gabe all but growled.

PJ nodded slowly. She knew he wanted to protect her, but she couldn't bring herself to allow it. She couldn't rely on him. No.

Any time she'd tried to depend on a man sticking around, it had gone horribly wrong. She'd fix this herself and then decide where her career would go from here. Maybe it was time to think about retiring. Or, at least slowing down a bit.

"I'll have Chad and Zach," she said quietly and slipped out from between Gabe and the counter, taking the first deep breath since she'd decided to tell him she needed to stand on her own two feet.

She ducked into the guest room and shut the door, leaning her head back against it as she let a few tears fall. She swiped at them and squeezed her eyes shut. She was doing the right thing —she was sure of it.

It might feel like she'd just been run over by a Mack truck, both emotionally and physically, but pulling away before he hurt her was the smart decision. And, PJ was all about trying to be smarter nowadays. She'd made enough stupid mistakes to last a lifetime.

Gabe didn't care what PJ said. He wouldn't be leaving her alone anytime soon. His car left his Connecticut home just moments after hers. They'd drive to the airport in separate cars, and he'd be flying a separate plane to Denver, but he'd be there as soon as she arrived. With any luck, he might get in ahead of her.

Shit. He knew he was beginning to look a bit like a stalker himself. In fact, if PJ knew how much he'd tried to match his own work schedule to her tour dates in the past; how much he'd kept an eye on her when she was staying at his hotels; how many extra little services he'd arranged for that had nothing to do with her VIP status and everything to do with his feelings for her, well shit. She probably would have run from him a lot faster than she had.

He wasn't sure when he'd started to fall for Pru. It hadn't been when they first met. He knew that. At the time, she'd been nineteen and he was twenty-nine. He was still heavily entrenched in building his chain of hotels, in beating back the memories of a ruined family he would never be able to recover, and she'd been just a sweet teenage pop star who stayed at his hotels. And then, one day, he'd looked up while attending a fundraiser, and she wasn't a teenager anymore. And, she no longer instilled sweet thoughts in him.

He had been about to approach her to say hello when one of his ex-girlfriends had swooped in and cut him off, hanging on his arm and draping herself over him in a drunken effort to hold his attention. But, what he'd noticed was Pru's look. She had looked at him...in a critical way. Like she knew the kind of man he was— a man who went through women faster than clean shirts—and her expression told him she wasn't interested in having anything to do with a man like that. He can't say he really blamed her. At the time, it was true—he dated a lot. A whole lot.

So he'd kept his distance. But, over time, they had talked when they found themselves at events together. He was drawn to her. Then, they started meeting on the rooftop gardens of the Towers where they talked a lot more. Got to know more about each other.

He had told her she could come up to his rooftop garden anytime he was in the hotel at the same time she was if she needed to escape the madness of her world, if she needed peace and privacy.

But now? Well, now he wanted more than occasional chats on rooftop gardens. He wanted to see where this would go with her. Good time or not, he wanted to pursue this relationship. And he sure as hell wouldn't walk away while she was in danger. He'd be there with her through this whether she wanted him there or not. And, in the end, he'd find a way to convince her he wasn't going anywhere. He wasn't going to move on to the next model or actress or whatever. He wanted Pru.

Chad and Zach knew Gabe planned to follow her back to the hotel. They couldn't do much to stop him, and it didn't appear as if she had asked them to do anything about it, so they let him do his thing.

He stepped out of the town car at the airport and strode up the steps to his private jet. He'd call Chad from the plane to be sure PJ got on her plane all right. She hadn't let him give her his jet to use so he'd arranged for her to borrow Jack's. He didn't want her flying commercial at a time like this. The press would be all over her, and she wouldn't have a minute's peace on a commercial flight.

CHAPTER 16

*P*ru followed Chad off the de Havilland jet, her guitar slung over one shoulder. She'd played a little on the flight, but she still felt as if she were somehow cut off from her music. It left a hollow ache in her stomach.

Zach flanked her and the steward carried her bag behind her. Her eyes landed immediately on the limousine and black SUV parked on the tarmac near the plane.

Well, those weren't exactly what her eyes fell on. No, they locked on Gabe who leaned casually against the limo, his long legs crossed and his phone in hand, looking like he was answering an email or text. Then he put his phone in his pocket and glanced up. He smiled and waved at her.

Waved. As though she hadn't told him she didn't want him there.

"Can we have a minute, guys?" Gabe asked, looking at Chad and Zach as PJ only stared at him. She had a feeling her jaw was on the ground, but she didn't care. The man just didn't give up.

As ticked off as she was about that, certain unmentionable girlie parts were doing a little happy dance over the same. But worse, her heart was skipping wildly in her chest. *Darn him.*

Chad and Zach nodded and stepped over to the SUV, while

Gabe opened the back door to the limo for her and ushered her inside. The privacy partition was up, separating the back of the car from the prying eyes and ears of the driver.

PJ waited for Gabe to explain himself, watching warily as his eyes pierced hers. He sighed and pulled her across the seat into his lap where she squirmed in response. He slapped a strong arm across her legs and locked her in place. "Keep that up and we won't be talking much longer, sweetheart," he growled.

She stilled. "Gabe, what part of 'I don't want you here' did you not understand?"

"PJ, I'm not Jimmy Mondo or that idiot, Kurt Tolleson. I'm not using you, and I'm not going to get bored and leave you. A long time ago, I thought the age difference between us would be a big deal, but now that we're older, the difference doesn't seem so big. I want to be with you. I want to make you happy and help you through this. And, after this is all over, I want to take time to get to know you and let you get to know me and see where this goes. But, I can already tell you where it's going for me."

She opened her mouth but he put his finger over it, cutting her off.

"I like you a whole lot more than any other woman I've ever been interested in. I love talking to you and hearing you laugh. And I love listening to you and finding out all the quirky things that make you tick." His eyes were open and honest and there was such emotion in them. Something she'd never seen with any of the men she'd been with before.

He looked down at her lips, and she saw heat flare in his eyes and felt the hard evidence of it beneath her—and that made her want to squirm in a different way.

"I love kissing you and holding you, and I know I'm going to love making love to you when we're ready for that. Even so, I'm not going to push you because I'm happy to wait until you're feeling right about this. But, what I'm not willing to do is leave you alone while you're dealing with so much and while you're still in danger. So don't ask me to, Pru."

PJ's emotions warred within her. She wanted to sink into his arms and let him hold her, but a very big part of her was afraid she was just turning herself over to another man the way she'd done with Jimmy and with Kurt. She'd given her all to them and in doing so, she had lost herself to them.

But, there was something else she'd felt with them that she didn't feel here. That she'd been searching for something. Reaching for what she thought she wanted. She'd wanted to feel love and to be loved so much that she didn't really question whether either was the right man for her. She was more in love with the idea of love with them.

With Gabe, she didn't feel that. She felt comfortable and safe and happy with him. He seemed to want her just as she was and on her terms. No pressure. She could be her own person when she was with him. She felt more turned on than she could have imagined she'd ever feel with a man.

PJ squirmed again, and Gabe groaned. "You have to stop that, Pru," he said, his hips raising a bit to grind his long hard length against her.

She gasped and stilled again, then nodded her head.

"Yes?" he asked.

"Yes," she said.

Gabe's mouth met hers, soft and warm and slowly seeking. She melted into him, opening herself up to him as he deepened the kiss and pulled her tightly to him. Everything in her sank into him, and she felt herself give up the last bit of resistance to him. She didn't want to fight him anymore. She wanted his strong arms around her, wanted him standing next to her in this and all the battles she would face down the road in life. She wanted him. *Wanted them.*

Gabe pressed a button and spoke to the driver, instructing him to head to the hotel. She tried to slide from his lap, but he didn't let her. One hand played in small circles on her thigh, causing her body to melt with need for him.

She wrapped her arms around him and lowered her head to his shoulder, relaxing for what felt like the first time in days. She didn't know if she was being smart, but she didn't care. There wasn't anywhere else she'd rather be at that moment than in his arms. Except perhaps, in his bed.

He read her mind. "You'll stay in my suite," he said.

She shook her head. "No. My team, the press, Gabe——" she started to say, but he squeezed her tighter.

"You'll stay with me."

She rolled her eyes. He may have asked her to continue to see where their relationship was going but apparently, he was back to being bossy and demanding again.

So, she'd stay with him. She shrugged internally. Who was she kidding? She *wanted* to stay with him. This was one time when she didn't care if he bossed her around.

PJ wasn't at all prepared for what she saw when they arrived on the rooftop of the Tower Hotel to check in with her team.

She rushed forward to where Ellis sat on a bench in handcuffs surrounded by police officers, and what she could only assume was Zach's security team that had come out ahead of them. Debra and Lydia looked on with shocked, pale faces and Ellis himself looked horrible. He'd been crying and looked so small as the officers towered over him.

"What are you doing to him? What's going on?" PJ demanded. This couldn't be happening.

She felt Gabe come up behind her, one hand on her shoulder as she knelt to see Ellis's face. He looked at her, tears streaking down his face.

"I'm sorry, PJ," was all he said. Ellis apologized over and

over as the police officers told PJ and the other new arrivals that Zach's men had found PJ's thumb drive with her journal on it in Ellis's luggage, complete with his fingerprints on the drive.

"No," PJ shook her head and stood to face the officers. "He didn't do this; he wouldn't do this." She was crying now as she looked to Debra and Lydia for help. "Lydia, you know he wouldn't do this."

Lydia shook her head. "I've called my mom. She's on her way with a lawyer. They're going to try to have him taken to a mental hospital instead of lockup tonight, or at least petition to have him transferred as soon as possible. He needs help, PJ."

PJ turned back to the officers. "I don't want to press charges." She probably sounded like a raving lunatic, but she knew in her heart it wasn't Ellis who had done this to her.

But if so, why wasn't he speaking up? Why wasn't he telling them he didn't do this? Why was he apologizing?

"I won't press charges," she said as Gabe put an arm around her.

"I'm sorry, ma'am," one of the officers said. "It's not up to you. He's a suspect in the murder of Jimmy Mondo. We've got to take him in."

Gabe leaned in and spoke quietly in PJ's ear. "Let's follow them over to the station and be sure his mom has a good lawyer for him. That's all we can do until this plays out, Pru."

She looked up at him and nodded, relieved to see in his eyes he believed her about Ellis's innocence. He believed Ellis didn't do this…. Well, maybe he didn't believe that in his heart the way she believed it in hers, but he was willing to listen to her and back Ellis up when she did.

And that meant more to PJ than she could ever say.

She knelt in front of Ellis again. "We're going to be right behind, you, okay? You're not going to be on your own in this, you hear me?"

He gave a shaky nod but his eyes were plastered to his lap. He wouldn't meet her gaze and that gutted her.

Chad came up to them and spoke quietly. "Samantha called. She's found Erika on video near your hotel in Indianapolis but nothing of her in any of the other overlapping cities. I'll share the information with the police," he said, looking over at Ellis. "For what it's worth."

Hope hit PJ. Maybe it was Erika the whole time, not Ellis. Gabe squeezed her hand.

PJ crossed to Debra while they waited for the officers to finish up and begin transporting Ellis.

"I did an interview on the flight over here," PJ told Debra. "I called Whitney Paulsen over at ZNN and did an exclusive with her. She's always been fair and a lot nicer to deal with than most reporters. I told her the whole story about Jimmy and the baby and the adoption. Since Matthew is all right with this coming out and Jimmy Mondo is dead, I felt I'd rather get it out in the open than continue to hide it. At least, that way, no one can hold this over me again."

Gabe's arms came around her from behind, and Debra smiled at her. "I think that was a smart move."

PJ nodded. "It was time. I should have been honest about it from the beginning. What Jimmy did was illegal. I should have dealt with the shame and been honest. I should have gone after him years ago for what he did."

"You shouldn't have done that," came Lydia's voice behind her.

PJ turned to her in confusion. Lydia's voice was cold and hard, but when all eyes turned to her, she smiled and waved off the questioning looks.

"I just mean you should have talked to Debra and me about it first. We should have coordinated that together as a team. We could have arranged for more coverage and turned things to your advantage a bit more. We can get a lot of mileage out of this."

PJ suppressed a sigh and looked at Ellis where he still sat handcuffed and waiting, an officer standing over him. He looked lost and confused and alone, and it broke her heart. "I don't want mileage out of this, Lydia. I want to get it out in the open and begin to live my life without secrets and fear and humiliation. I'm not looking to profit from this."

Lydia shook her head. "No, of course not. I'm sorry, PJ. I should have thought before I blurted that out. I shouldn't have said anything."

PJ watched as the officers helped Ellis stand, his hands still cuffed behind his back. His voice shook as he spoke, seemingly to no one in particular.

"Why didn't she love me?" he asked and PJ's heart broke for him. He turned teary eyes to his sister who looked back at him, her expression blank. "Why, Lydia, why?"

CHAPTER 17

*G*abe stayed by PJ's side as they made their way to the police station. Ellis's mom arrived shortly after and the attorney she had with her appeared to be more than competent.

The attorney had the officers put Ellis on suicide watch, and said his office was already initiating the motions needed to push to have Ellis moved to a secure mental health facility as soon as possible. The attorney wasn't sure they'd win, but he was willing to try.

PJ was beside herself when the officers told them he'd be moved to the county jail within a few hours. There were statements to take and reports to write up and then, when the formalities were finished, he'd be transferred.

Even Gabe had a hard time thinking of Ellis in prison and he barely knew him. He truly hoped PJ was right that it wasn't Ellis, and they'd be able to find a way to clear his name and get him released quickly.

Gabe also noticed the strange dynamic between Lydia and her mom. Her mother seemed to treat Lydia as if she were just another part of PJ's team, rather than her daughter.

Lydia made sure the officers had Ellis's insulin for his diabetes maintenance and released a statement to the press in a businesslike manner, but other than that, there didn't appear to be any sisterly concern for Ellis at all. But, Pru had said Lydia was like that. Like a machine. He just hadn't realized she meant it quite so literally.

By the time they returned to his suite and left Chad and Zach out in the living room watching over things, he knew Pru was completely wiped out. She'd have to do interviews in the morning to respond to the questions about why one of her team had been arrested, and to respond to all of the questions that would come now that the story about Matthew's biological parentage had gone out.

Lydia had responded to a few of the reporters' questions outside the police station, but there would be more to answer in the coming days.

Gabe left Pru sitting on the edge of his bed and stepped into the bathroom to draw her a hot bath. He added a squeeze of the bath gel his hotel supplied from their spa line of beauty products and tested the temperature with his hand.

When he went back to the bedroom to get PJ, she just watched him with wide eyes as he pulled her into the bathroom and stripped her clothes off. She was beautiful and soft and warm.

Part of him wanted nothing more than to wrap himself around her and bury himself to the hilt in her hot, sweet body, but it was obvious she didn't need that right now. She looked positively wrecked.

All he wanted to do was take care of her. To take the stunned, beaten look off her face.

He held her hand as she sat down in the tub, but when he tried to draw away to get a washcloth, she didn't let go of his hand.

"Come in with me," she whispered. "Please?" she begged before he could say no—and he couldn't deny her. Hell, he didn't want to. As much as he didn't want to push her into anything, he couldn't hold back any longer. Not when she looked at him like that. Like he was the only thing in the world she needed.

The water splashed and rose up to the top of the bath when he stepped in, but he pulled her around, settling her into his arms, nestled between his legs.

His cock was hard and practically screaming with frustration, but he wrapped his arms around her and began rubbing the tight muscles in her arms and shoulders. He let his hands trail down her arms and brush forward to her breasts—full, luscious breasts that peeked out through the bubbles that floated on top of the hot water.

As her nipples hardened under his fingers, she gasped, and his name came out on a long moan.

Gabe couldn't get enough. She pressed against his hard length—God what he wouldn't do to slip inside her slick heat and make love to her hot and hard. But not yet.

She laid her head back against him and turned it, letting him capture her mouth in his. Nothing had ever felt this incredible. He'd never wanted anything to last so long, to go on endlessly. He wanted PJ in his arms forever.

Gabe let one hand travel down her stomach, between her legs where she was so slick and swollen. All for him. When his fingers pressed into her, she gasped against his mouth, and he heard himself moaning now.

God, how he wanted this woman. He'd meant to take this slow, but there wasn't any stopping this. She wriggled back against him, pressing closer still, pushing her ass back into him until he grew harder and thicker. So ready for her.

PJ twisted, and he drew his legs closer together, knowing what she wanted. As she straddled him, he knew they needed to get out of the tub. He needed to get her into his bedroom where he could get to a condom, but it appeared she had other things in mind.

PJ glided back and forth over him, the heat of her body driving him mad as he let himself get lost in those eyes. She could torment him forever, and if he died, he'd die a happy man.

Gabe's hands found her breasts again, rubbing his fingers softly over the peaked nipples, pinching her lightly...drawing that moan from her again. It ended on a whimper.

"I want you inside me," she said and Gabe pushed her back to rise out of the tub, then pulled her out of the water with him. They fell onto the bed dripping wet and tangled, but he managed to reach for his bag next to the nightstand and felt through it until he found the box of condoms he'd stashed in there before leaving his house. It seemed like a million years ago.

Her eyes were on his, trusting and open, as he sheathed himself and then pressed his cock to her wet slit...seeking. He teased back and forth and watched her mouth open in a silent moan, and her heavy-lidded eyes close halfway at the sensation.

He pressed inside, wishing the amazing feeling of entering her for the first time could last forever, go on forever.

He didn't move quickly...but wasn't slow either. His body needed to be inside her all the way. To his amazement, her warmth wrapped around him, milking him. He lay his forehead on hers and paused, just soaking in the sensations, feeling her so tight around him.

"You feel incredible, Pru. All for me," he said and she nodded.

"All for you," she said as her hips began to move, and he thought his eyes would roll to the back of his head with the pleasure she gave him.

PJ couldn't stay still. Gabe filled her so completely, making her wild with the need to feel more, feel everything as sensations rained down on her. His mouth was on her lips, then her neck, then her breasts as she became more swollen, more wet with need.

He drove into her again and again, and she knew, somehow, it would never be enough. She would never tire of him, of this connection to him.

"Gabe," she moaned as he drew back and teased her with shorter strokes, drawing out the pleasure rushing through her. His hand dropped between them and his fingers found her clit, pressing, circling, driving her mad.

Her muscles clamped down on him as she felt herself fall over the edge in what seemed like record time. He pushed deep and hard and long again, abandoning the small strokes, filling her as he came with her.

When the aftershocks left her system, she wrapped her arms around Gabe where he'd fallen half on top of her, half to the side as if he held his weight off her.

"Relax. I won't break," she said and pulled him down closer. He groaned, but sank onto her. The weight of him felt good. Reassuring in some way.

God, she already felt so much for this man. So much it scared her when she thought about it. So she tried not to. She wouldn't let what had happened with Jimmy Mondo and Kurt Tolleson spoil this for her.

Gabe rose up, leaned on one elbow and looked into her eyes. She felt vulnerable, like he could see everything she was thinking, and more.

"Any regrets?" he whispered, kissing the knuckles of the hand he held in his.

She shook her head. "No."

"Ready to do that again?" he asked.

He dropped his head to her breasts, beginning a trail that led him under the covers, and that took her breath away again, just as quickly as she'd gotten it back. And it was quickly obvious he wasn't kidding about doing it again.

CHAPTER 18

The call came at five am, waking them both. There had been a screw-up at the prison.

When Ellis had been transferred to the county lockup from the local precinct, somehow the suicide watch hadn't been communicated. At three am, Ellis hanged himself using strips of his prison sheets.

Gabe held PJ as she cried, and he spoke quietly to her, telling her it would be all right, but he knew it wouldn't be. Her heart was breaking, and he didn't know how to fix it.

Ellis left a note with only the words 'I'm so sorry, PJ' written on it. The officer who called them believed the note was proof of his guilt, and he knew the rest of the team would believe that as well. The police felt he'd been so guilt-ridden over what he'd done to PJ and to Jimmy that he'd taken his own life.

Gabe had seen the look in PJ's eyes when she heard the words he'd written. She didn't want to think Ellis had done this, but he saw in her eyes that she was beginning to believe he had. That maybe it had been faithful, loyal, so-in-love-with-her Ellis all this time.

It made sense. He'd had a crush on her for so long. Gabe

suspected he'd seen her putting her journal away at some point and had stolen it. Probably to see if she ever wrote about Ellis. And, instead, he'd found out her biggest secret. That she'd given up a child just as his own mother had done to him.

The one thing Ellis hadn't learned from the journal was Matt's true identity. PJ always wrote about Matthew as her cousin. She wrote about her birth child and how she missed him, missed holding him and seeing him every day, but she didn't connect the two up in her journal.

She had told Gabe it was a way to protect herself a bit. Never letting herself think of Matthew as that child. As hers. It allowed her to love him in the way she needed to: as her cousin, not her son.

Still, with the timeline and her cousin's age, it wasn't hard to think the tabloids would have put two and two together and come up with Matthew once they knew there was a baby out there.

PJ took a deep, shuddering breath. "Do you think it was him? Was it Ellis all this time?" she asked, as though reading his thoughts.

"I don't know, sweetheart. I'd like to think he wouldn't have done this, but something made him say he was sorry. Something drove him to kill himself. Guilt is a pretty powerful thing. Maybe he couldn't reconcile loving you and hating you all at the same time. Loving the you he'd known all these years, but hating that you'd given up a child. Chad said Ellis's early years were really hard. He'd been in a lot of foster homes, and even a group home situation before Lydia's parents adopted him. To him, the happy ending you were able to find with Matthew's adoption didn't seem possible."

"I just don't want to think he could have done this. He's always been there for me. Even though he knew I didn't feel the same way for him that he did for me, he was always my friend. He was always so good. I can't see him taking a life. Even someone like Jimmy. The Ellis I knew wasn't capable of that."

"Maybe he saw Jimmy as the reason you gave up Matthew. If he hadn't pushed for the abortion so hard, if he hadn't gotten such a young girl pregnant, you wouldn't have had to do what you did. It could be that it was hard for Ellis to blame you for it since he's loved you all this time, but easier to turn that rage on Jimmy."

Gabe kissed her temple. "Try to get some rest, honey. We probably won't ever know why he did any of this. You need to rest."

She closed her eyes, but he felt her tears continue to fall, and all he could do was hold her tightly, until finally, she fell asleep.

They traveled to Ellis's mom's home in Massachusetts for the funeral. Chad returned to Connecticut, but Zach and two of his people stayed on. They'd be staying with PJ until they put new security in place—security vetted by both Zach and Chad.

Gabe watched as PJ spoke quietly to Ellis's mom after the funeral when they'd all returned to the house. Ellis's mother smiled weakly and nodded, and Gabe knew PJ was doing her best to comfort her.

He had also seen a more human side to Lydia during the funeral trip. Oh, she had been a whirlwind, organizing the funeral service, the catering for the after-funeral get-together, ensuring notices got in the paper.... That type of thing.

But, Lydia had also been there to console her mom. He watched now as Lydia and PJ walked arm in arm up the stairs. Lydia said she would gather some photos of Ellis for PJ to take with her, so he assumed that's where they were headed.

Their heads were bowed together as they murmured to one another.

This had to be hard on Lydia, even if she had sometimes treated Ellis more like an employee than a brother. But, Gabe had never worked with family, so maybe that was necessary to keep things running smoothly at work.

Gabe left Zach by the buffet table and wandered into the den off the living room. There were a few people here and there in the room, talking in small groups, but it was much less crowded than the living room. He took in the walls lined with family photos.

There were dozens of them. They seemed to go in mostly chronological order, beginning on the left side of the room when Lydia was just an infant. Gabe looked at the photos and continued to the point where Lydia must have been about fourteen years old. It struck Gabe as odd how often Lydia was being held by her father in the photos. Even in all of the early pictures where she was a tiny infant, she was in her father's arms, not her mother's. Perhaps her mom was the photographer in the family....

When Lydia was about fourteen years old, someone else entered the pictures. There was Ellis grinning at the camera, always next to his mother. In fact, in many of them, Ellis stood between his mother and Lydia instead of one child on either side of their mother.

The family dynamic was incredibly bizarre, and the preferences were more than a little evident to anyone looking at them. Over time, Lydia stood a little further away from Ellis and her mother, rarely smiling. It was subtle, but unmistakable.

Gabe wondered how Lydia's mom could make such a showcase of the photos. He would have thought she'd hide the photos away. Or at the very least, that she would have noticed what the pictures showed over the years—that she preferred her son—and made changes. But, apparently she hadn't.

The information was there in color for him, the whole story laid out. For a couple of pictures after Ellis arrived, there were Lydia and her father and Ellis and his mother. They all stood together in the photos, but they were separate at the same time. Each parent clearly doting on their 'chosen' child.

And then Lydia's father was gone. A car accident, Gabe remembered. From then on, it was only Lydia by herself, standing next to her mother and Ellis, so clearly separated from them by some invisible wall. Lydia also appeared extremely angry, and all of that anger was directed at one person. *Ellis.*

In almost every shot, Lydia was ignored. She stood off to the side in many, her gaze intent on one thing: her brother with her mom. Good God, even at Lydia's own high school graduation, Ellis and his mom stood slightly apart from Lydia in the picture. She looked at the camera, but her expression was off. As though she knew she stood alone.

Ellis, on the other hand, looked adoringly at his sister. If her mom hadn't noticed her lack of love for her brother, apparently neither had he.

Gabe shook himself. Maybe he was being silly—reading much more into these pictures than was really there. But, the hair on the back of his neck stood on end, and he suddenly wanted to get to Pru.

He strode from the room and crossed through the living room in a few strides, grabbing Zach as he went. They took the stairs at a run, and that's when he heard it. The sound of glass breaking upstairs.

Gabe picked up speed.

He wasn't prepared for what he saw when he burst into the room. PJ and Lydia knelt on the floor over a broken picture frame. But what really hit him, was PJ's arms around Lydia as sobs wracked the other woman's body.

He and Zach backed out of the room and went downstairs to wait for the women to join them. They came down an hour later as the last of the guests left. PJ and her team said their good-byes, and PJ gave Lydia a final hug on the front steps.

In the morning, PJ and her team would go on to the next stop on the tour, resuming the schedule that had been interrupted two days before. Debra would take over for Lydia for the next few stops until she was ready to rejoin them on the tour.

CHAPTER 19

*G*abe was silent as he removed his clothing, before swiftly stripping PJ of hers. Even though he'd been wrong about Lydia, he hadn't fully recovered from the icy fear that raced through his veins when he'd thought Lydia might be the real person trying to hurt PJ.

His hands had shaken, and his heart pounded when he thought she was in danger.

He'd never needed to hold her and love her more than he needed that now. He wanted to sink into her and just hold on, make love to her for hours.

He sat on the edge of the bed and pulled her into his lap, impaling her in one swift stroke as she sank onto him. She groaned and wrapped her arms around his neck, letting her head fall to his shoulder.

He began to move slowly within her, pumping his hips slightly as he leaned down to capture a nipple in his mouth, drawing another moan from her.

Gabe caught her arms in his and held them behind her back, pushing her breasts closer to him, exposing her, so he could worship every inch of her body. She kept her arms still as he let his free hand glide down her body, hips pumping all the while, reveling in the feel of her muscles surrounding him, drawing out every inch of pleasure.

"You feel so incredible, so right, Pru."

She drew her arms forward, wrapping them around his neck again and began her own dance upon him, speeding up the circles with her hips as he gritted his teeth, holding on as long as he could. Gabe slid one hand to her clit, circling, while the other tugged gently at a nipple, knowing that would set her loose.

Her muscles rippled immediately, and she cried out, clamping down on him. He ground his hips against hers, drawing their orgasms out as she collapsed onto his shoulder.

When the aftershocks ended, he lay back on the bed, hugging her to him, scooting them up to the pillows.

"You thought Lydia was going to hurt me, didn't you?" PJ asked when they both had caught their breath. She raised her head and looked at him as he nodded.

"It turns out," she said, "she's been holding herself together this whole time by throwing herself into making the arrangements and taking care of her mom. She's torn up about losing Ellis, and doesn't feel she can turn to her mom because her mother's grieving herself."

"Then I'm glad you were able to be there for her," Gabe said, brushing his hand over her wild curls. "You sure you're ready to return to the stage tomorrow, babe? You sure you're not pushing too fast, too much?"

PJ paused, not sure how much to tell him about what she'd been thinking lately.

"That doesn't sound very sure," he said with a laugh, but she heard his concern.

"It's not tomorrow that's got me thinking. It's the end of the tour."

He leaned up on one elbow and looked at her as she spoke, one arm stroking her shoulder.

"When the tour ends next month, I'm not sure I want to book

another one. I think maybe it's time to retire. Or, at least take a break. Write at my own pace, release stuff on the Internet when I feel like it – or not, when I don't feel like it."

"What brought this on?" Gabe asked.

She shrugged a shoulder. "I think I've been winding down for a while now, but honestly, having the last week off has been really nice. I want to do other things right now. Like make friends." She paused to kiss him before continuing.

"I want to spend more time with Matthew, make sure we're okay. I want to spend more time with you," she said, a flush telling him she wasn't sure he'd want that, too.

"I want nothing more than to spend time with you too," he said. "But not unless you're sure it's what you want. I can follow you to most of your tour stops. Jack's already started the process to sell my company. All that really needs to be done is to settle on terms and take care of due diligence. That'll keep me busy for a bit, but my assistant and her team are set up to handle a lot of that workload for me. You don't need to stop touring to be with me."

She smiled. "It means a lot that you'd do that for me, but I think this is what I want. I think I'm finished. I've been on the road almost nonstop since I was fifteen. I think it's time to settle into a different life. Besides, didn't you say Jack had an offer for you? Some new project to keep you busy after you sell the hotels?"

He nodded. "He wants me to come work at Sutton with him, advising start-up companies, helping to tweak their business plans in the first year of business, that kind of thing. It'll be interesting. I'll get to work with different types of companies, be in on the exciting stages at start-up and then move on to something new. But, I'd only want to do that if you were living in Connecticut with me. If you wanted to be there with me," he clarified.

She straddled him again and smiled down on him while her

hair fell over her naked shoulders and breasts. "There's nowhere else I'd rather be."

"Then, that's settled," Gabe said. "We finish out this tour, then head back to Connecticut."

She nodded, her smile wide, but then a shadow crossed her face.

"I do worry about Lydia and the band. This means forcing them to find other jobs. I feel guilty," she admitted.

Gabe shook his head. "You can't live your life for other people, honey. It's one thing to worry about other people and be considerate of their feelings. It's another to live a life you don't want because of their needs. You can't let yourself feel guilty for living the life you need after so many years on the road."

"Yeah," she whispered, letting her head fall back down to his chest. He felt her yawn and pulled the comforter up over them.

"Sleep, Pru," he whispered and let his hands go back to rubbing her shoulders until he heard her breathing even out.

CHAPTER 20

*P*J looked up from her phone to see Lydia striding toward her, a bag slung over her shoulder, her take-charge look set firmly on her face.

The only thing was, PJ hadn't expected to see Lydia this morning. The plan had been for the group to go ahead to the next few tour stops without her. Debra would take over Lydia's duties so she could spend a few more days with her mom. In fact, they'd told her to take all the time she needed after Ellis's death.

"Lydia," PJ said, as the other woman drew close to where PJ and Gabe stood next to the tour bus. "What are you doing here? You should be with your family."

The other woman's smile was tight, and PJ's heart twisted in her chest for this woman she'd never really seen as a friend, but felt for all the same.

"My mom doesn't need me right now, and I'd feel better just getting back to work. I need to keep myself busy."

PJ nodded, and they waited quietly for the rest of the team to assemble. It wasn't the right time to tell Lydia that this would be her last tour. She would hold off on that and let Lydia bury herself in work if that's what she needed.

PJ had a lot of contacts in the industry, and Lydia was well known and respected for her ability to handle anything and everything that was thrown at her on a tour. With PJ's help, she'd have a number of jobs to choose from when the tour ended.

Gabe's arm came around PJ, and she smiled up at him as they slipped into the SUV they'd be taking to the airport. There would be sound checks and makeup and hair prep to sit through. After over a week of just throwing on moisturizer and lip gloss and mascara, PJ knew sitting through the hours of makeup and hair wouldn't be easy.

Gabe wrapped his arms around her, and she snuggled into him for the drive to the airport. They'd fly to Denver and go straight to the venue for the show before even checking into the hotel.

PJ sighed.

Yup.

She was finished with this life. It was time to say good-bye.

CHAPTER 21

*G*abe barely kept his hands to himself as they made their way to the hotel after the show. He loved the version of Pru he'd been with the past week—with her laid-back style and the light makeup she'd worn each day.

But, he had to say, there was also something compelling about the vixen she became when she performed on stage. Her eyes were done in smoky tones making her that much more bewitching to him. She wore red heels with deep-blue, sequined jeans and a red top that flowed around her curves and hid silken, milky skin that he knew would taste sweet when he finally got his mouth on her.

Her jeans showed him things about her body his hands wanted to learn as well, and he had no desire to wait a minute longer than he had to.

It was agonizing to watch her perform under the lights tonight, because he wanted to haul her off the stage and press her up against the wall on more than one occasion. And she knew it, too. Through the night, she'd looked over and given him a cheeky wink, or an extra flick of her hips when the choreography of her show brought her to his side of the stage.

As they entered their hotel suite, he pressed her up against the wall, pinning her between himself and the door. He'd asked Zach's guys to stay in a separate room until they needed them later, knowing he'd want privacy for a good long while.

PJ laughed a husky, dangerous laugh as he lifted her, wrapping her legs around his waist and pressing her into the wall, pulling at her shirt. He had a driving need somehow to bind her to him. To mark her and make her his.

He didn't care when he heard the fabric of her shirt tear under his hands, and she didn't seem to either. She'd told him once that after a show, she was cranked up and pumped full of adrenaline for hours, and he could feel that now as she kissed him back, her fingers grasping his hair and tugging as she tried to pull him even closer.

Gabe walked to the couch with Pru still clinging to him, not willing to break the connection in any way. She slid down his body. As her feet came to rest on the floor, he turned her away from him and quickly removed the rest of her shirt.

If you asked Gabe if he could ever be utterly enthralled by a woman's back before, he would have said no. Sure, looking at a woman's curvy figure from the back held some appeal, but he'd never imagined it could be like this.

She was a goddess before him, quivering at his touch, as he worshiped her shoulders, the curve on the side of her neck, the slope of her breasts that peeked out along the sides of her body.

When he undid her jeans and slid his hand down her stomach to her center, the place he needed to lose himself in, she was wet and swollen and pressed herself into his hand, grinding against him—her own need as great as his. Gabe moaned and tore the jeans down her hips, taking her lace panties with them.

Their lovemaking wasn't slow and easy and tender. It was hard and fast and raw. Gabe's arousal was heightened by the sight of Pru bent over the couch as he entered her from behind, his hand tangled in her hair, pulling to give her that tiny bite of pain that drove her wild beneath him.

God, the vision of her was intoxicating as he spilled into her, plunging again and again while her orgasm ripped through her beautiful body.

CHAPTER 22

*G*abe lifted PJ and carried her to the bedroom where they lay, a tangle of arms and legs, breathing heavily, both trying to recover. PJ ran her hands over Gabe's back, loving the feel of his muscles beneath her hands.

He was nothing short of absolute perfection, and a small part of her still couldn't believe this was real. That he was here, with her. That he *wanted* to be here with her.

Another part of her couldn't believe how incredible sex was with him, and she had to bite her lip at the thought to hold back a laugh. Being with Jimmy and Kurt hadn't come close to what it was like with Gabe.

It was as though every cell in her body was tuned to his body, every inch of her made for him and him for her. The thrill of it – of his touch, his taste, of the orgasms he sent screaming through her body – was addictive, and she knew she'd give anything to hold onto him forever.

"Tell me more about your family," she said, running her hands in light lines up his back, then down again.

Gabe kissed her slowly before drawing back and turning to look up at the ceiling.

"What do you want to know?" he asked. It was his turn to run his fingers over her now, his hand brushing the skin on her arm as she snuggled into his side.

"What was your sister like? Were you close to her?" Pru was an only child, but she couldn't imagine the pain of losing a sister and a parent at once.

"Mandy? Yeah, I loved her," he said with a small smile. "She was three years younger than me, so there were times when she was a pain in my—"

"Hey!" PJ cut him off swatting his arm. "Not nice."

He grinned, then his face grew soft and serious. "But I loved her. I'd have done anything for her. When I came home from school for visits, we'd hang out when I wasn't seeing friends. Just get ice cream and sit on the hood of my car in the parking lot of DQ and talk about how school was going for her and what schools she wanted to apply to. Or what Mom and Dad were doing to drive her nuts that week." He shrugged a shoulder. "That kind of thing."

"I'm so sorry she's gone, Gabe," PJ whispered.

"Me too," he whispered back and kissed her gently. "She would have loved you."

PJ's heart flipped in her chest at the thought of all he had missing from his life now. Here she'd been, so jealous of the tight bonds he had with his friends, but he'd lost his sister and father, and he'd told her his mother's mind was slipping away more and more with each passing day.

"How often do you see your mom?"

This brought another shrug from him, but she knew he cared a lot more than he was letting on. "Once a month. More if I can. She only recognizes me now every few visits. It's awful to say, but sometimes I think it'll be a blessing when she dies. She's in a really good facility that specializes in dementia, but honestly, she began to slip away the minute my father and sister were gone. I don't think she wants to be here without them. I think part of her always wished she went with them."

PJ framed his face with her hands and kissed him long and gently, willing away the feelings of sorrow she could see on his face as she did. She'd give anything to take away that pain for him. His arms came around her and pulled her on top of him, and she felt herself sink into the kiss, hoping he would lose himself in her body until the sad memories left him.

CHAPTER 23

*O*ver the course of the next few days, Gabe tried to tell himself to relax. That the immediate threat to Pru was gone. Her secrets were out to the world and Ellis couldn't hurt her any longer. But, when he thought about the fact that Jimmy had lost his life in all of this, it hit home just how vulnerable Pru was. Ellis could have killed her.

They'd gotten the final reports on a lot of the missing details and the picture of what had happened was becoming clearer. Jimmy Mondo's blood alcohol level had been below the legal limit, but he'd had high doses of a date rape drug in his system.

The police theorized it had been slipped into his drink just before he left the bar. It wouldn't have kicked in until he was already behind the wheel driving home.

The bandmate who suffered numerous miscarriages had been exactly where she said she'd been when Jimmy had been killed. More than one person had verified that she'd spent those days in New York City with friends.

Gabe's hotel hadn't found Lydia on the video footage in any of the public areas of the hotel, so her whereabouts were still a little murky, but the police had shared more information on Ellis's case with Chad.

Ellis had a lot of photos of Pru on his phone. Everyone had known he had a crush on her, but the photos made it clear it went beyond a passing crush. It had been an obsession. And, in addition to finding the USB drive in his luggage, there had been a burner phone in there as well. The same burner phone that had been used to text the threatening messages to Pru.

As harmless as everyone wanted to think Ellis had been, he'd turned out to be hiding a very dark personality behind his meek facade.

But, what still ate at Gabe was the fact that Pru remained vulnerable as long as she was such a public figure. There were other weirdoes out there. Her secrets might be out in the open, making it impossible to hold them over her again, but that wouldn't necessarily stop some crazed fan from going after her....

Gabe had to admit he was more than a little relieved she'd decided to step back from touring for a while. He'd feel better when they were just two normal people living an ordinary, everyday existence in Connecticut.

Oh, he got that she could never be obscure. Her fame was a part of who she was and would be a part of her forever, but if she stepped back from the limelight, he'd at least feel like she wasn't as big a target anymore. Wouldn't be as out there to the world.

His phone buzzed and he glanced down at it. He was sitting outside the venue of Pru's show, catching up on emails and messages from his assistant. Pru and Lydia were tucked inside the tour bus that idled in the alley next to the venue, working on last-minute changes to her schedule.

He'd grab her for an early dinner in about thirty minutes. Some days, if no one made sure she ate, she didn't. Ironically, it used to be Ellis who always made sure she had her meals.

"Hey, Chad," Gabe said, closing his laptop as he answered the phone.

Chad didn't bother with a greeting, and the tone of his voice set Gabe on edge. What he said sent his blood running cold.

"Lydia's mom was discovered dead in her bed this morning. The police believe she died two days ago, the evening of Ellis's funeral."

Gabe was up and moving as Chad continued.

"The police initially thought it was suicide, but one of the officers was paying close attention and realized the glass of juice she had next to her bed had powder residue in it, as though the pills from the empty bottle of valium next to her had been crushed and put in the juice, not swallowed whole. Or, as though someone gave her a small dose in the juice to disorient her, and then force-fed the others once she was out of it. They haven't said conclusively yet whether it was murder or suicide, but if it was murder, there's only one suspect." Chad didn't have to tell Gabe who that was.

"Lydia," Gabe said.

"The police are on the way. Is PJ with you?"

Gabe didn't answer. He'd dropped his phone. He couldn't just wait for the police to arrive. Not when Pru was inside the tour bus, alone, with Lydia. He needed to get her out of there.

He waved to Zach's guys—Justice and Eric—who had been told to take a break nearby and quickly filled them in on the situation. They were on the same page as he was—try to get Pru out of there before the police arrived, and the whole thing got a hell of a lot more complicated.

Gabe headed to the side entrance of the tour bus, the one that would lead into the living room space, while the others made their way to the back of the bus, toward the sleeping quarters. Justice and Eric were two of Zach's best men, but Gabe's world still slowed to a crawl as he opened the door to the bus.

PJ knew at some point she'd come clean with Lydia; tell her

they'd focused on her for part of the investigation into who was blackmailing her, and who had killed Jimmy.

As they sat in the tour bus going through the schedule of added interviews she would do in response to all that had happened in the last week, guilt gnawed at her stomach. She felt she should confess that they'd gone so far as to try to pinpoint her location during the time of the murder.

Gabe and Chad would probably tell her she shouldn't feel any guilt because they needed to find out who was trying to hurt her. At the time, they'd had to do whatever it took to keep her safe. But, now that she and Lydia were spending more time together, now that Lydia seemed to be turning more toward PJ in her grief over Ellis's death, PJ felt almost like she'd betrayed her friend.

True, the betrayal had happened before the friendship truly grew, but she'd known Lydia since they were kids. PJ should have been more loyal and sure of her.

But, look at where her loyalty toward Ellis had got her. That loyalty had apparently been completely misplaced.

PJ opened her mouth to speak, to say what she felt she needed to so they could put it behind them, but the door to the bus opened before she could say a word. Gabe stood in the doorway, taking in the two of them as they sat side by side on the couch.

"Hey, ladies. Peej, you got a minute?" he asked, his eyes glancing from Lydia to PJ and back again.

Why was he calling her Peej? He never did that.

And, that's when PJ felt it. Not just the crackle of tension that somehow seemed to fill the air. Not the *whoosh* of her own breath leaving her, or the ever-so-slight shift in Lydia from friend to threat that happened in the blink of an eye.

It was the sharp jab in her ribs she felt most acutely....

The other things all seemed to follow immediately thereafter, as the world slowed down. Lydia's voice came to her as though

158 | LORI RYAN

she were speaking in a tunnel, echoing and slower than it should have been.

"No, Gabe," Lydia said with a sick smile crossing her face. "She doesn't have a minute. She's not going anywhere."

Gabe lost the smile as his eyes narrowed on Lydia. He stepped further into the bus, hands held out at his waist, showing he wasn't a threat.

"Stop there," Lydia said, and PJ looked down at her side to confirm what she felt.

The barrel of a gun dug into her ribcage.

Gabe stood in the doorway to the living area. PJ was closest to him, but with the gun right at her side, there was no way she could move, no way could she get away from Lydia.

And, with PJ between him and Lydia, there was no way for him to tackle Lydia or do anything to help her. They were both utterly at a disadvantage.

"What—?" she started, but Lydia twisted and jabbed at her ribs, causing her to stop.

"Your boyfriend isn't very good at hiding his emotions, is he?"

Lydia laughed but there wasn't any humor in the sound. There was just anger and hatred, the kind that only came with a twisted soul.

"It's just like you, PJ," she practically spat out. "Just like you to walk away from all of this with the world thinking you're some kind of saint for being brave enough to give up your child; you get to go right back to your career, *and* you get the man. Good god," she laughed bitterly. "You're walking out of this with everything you came into it with, and a gorgeous billionaire who fucking loves you."

PJ shook her head, but Lydia sneered at her and continued. "You and Ellis are just alike. Always doted on. Always loved. Always having every damned thing you want handed to you as though you're somehow better than the world around you."

"I don't think Ellis had anything handed to him," PJ said,

unable to stop the honest assessment from coming out of her mouth. "He had a horrible life in foster care before he came to your family."

Ellis of all people had never asked the world for anything. All PJ had ever seen him do was give and care and love the people around him, even Lydia.

The gun dug into her again sharply and PJ sucked in a breath.

"No!" screamed Lydia, making PJ jump. "He used that, used his history to manipulate *everyone* into loving him, doting on him. It was all part of the show he put on for the world. The poor Ellis White show he'd perfected over the years."

Lydia turned her attention back to Gabe. "What was it that gave it all away?" Her tone was more idle curiosity than anything else, and it struck PJ as so utterly at odds with what was happening.

How quickly Lydia had downshifted from the anger rolling off her in waves only a moment before when she'd been talking about Ellis. She was truly sick.

The realization shook PJ. They weren't dealing with a stable person at all, and that scared her more than anything.

Gabe seemed to understand what Lydia was asking, but PJ felt dazed as she tried to follow their conversation.

"Got a call from the police back in Massachusetts," Gabe said, sounding calmer than PJ felt. "It seems your mom hasn't been answering phone calls or the door. At first, everyone assumed she was just upset, that she needed time to deal with the loss of her son. But after a couple of days, one of the neighbors finally used the key she had given him to go in and check on the house when she was out of town. Despite the fact that you cranked the air conditioning in her house, the smell when he entered gave it away."

PJ swallowed as Gabe turned to her, his voice trying to portray calm, as though he wasn't concerned about the situation. "Lydia fed her mother a lethal dose of valium the night of Ellis's funeral.

She put the first dose in a glass of orange juice. Did you force the rest of the pills down her throat after she was unconscious, Lydia?"

Lydia sneered again but didn't answer.

PJ closed her eyes. *This couldn't be happening. It could not be happening. Oh god. Ellis.*

She opened her eyes and stared at Lydia. "You set Ellis up. He had nothing to do with this, did he?" she asked.

"Nothing? Are you kidding? He had *everything* to do with this. Everything. He was the one who started it all. He came into our family and changed it all. He took my parents away from me with his never-ending need for love, for validation, for attention. My dad tried to balance things out, to be sure I didn't get lost when my mom turned all her love to Ellis, but then my dad died and I was left alone."

Lydia had lost all semblance of calm. She was shrieking now. "And, my mom...my mom never cared about me. Never really had when I think back on it. But, she loved Ellis. God, how she loved Ellis. When she demanded I help get him this job, I knew I'd never get away from him, he'd never stop ruining everything good in my life. I finally have a career I love, that I'm good at— and when I go home and tell her what I'm doing, she says, 'Ellis could do that with you.'"

PJ just stared. Ellis had to be interviewed the same as all of the other applicants for the job he'd held. Sure, he'd gotten the interview based on his relationship to Lydia, but he'd qualified for that job fair and square. And, he'd been good at it. He'd been a crucial part of PJ's team in the past six months.

"Then you start in with Ellis just like my mom. Always defending him. Always sticking up for him like he was some big part of the team, like we needed him here."

"Why now?" Gabe asked, drawing PJ from the thoughts that swirled in her head.

"Ah," Lydia said. "That was Ellis, too. You see, he isn't innocent in any of this at all," she said. "Ellis was the one who stole your journal. At least the first time."

There was a subtle shift in Gabe's face—it was there and gone in a flash, causing PJ to wonder if she'd imagined it. Lydia was still focused on PJ and her diatribe about Ellis and showed no sign that she'd seen the shift in his expression.

"He watched you all the time. When you thought you were alone, Ellis was there. He went so far as to put a tiny spy cam in one of your bags. Did you know that? Did you know the little creep was spying on you? He saw you writing in it, and he hid to watch where you put it away. You didn't know the little creep was that obsessed with you, did you? He stole it to see if you ever wrote about him."

The laugh and smirk on her lips were cruel and twisted.

"He cried when he discovered your secret; that you were as bad as his slut mother who didn't want him. I told him to put the flash drive back and forget he'd read it. You know, despite that, it still took him over a week to realize it was me when your journal was leaked to the press. He puffed up all righteous and told me I had to stop. When I reminded him he started it all, he broke down and cried, begged me to stop."

PJ didn't care what Ellis had done. He didn't deserve to die for it and she had no doubt Lydia had something to do with pushing him to take his own life. Lydia continued her warped diatribe before PJ could say anything.

"It was easy to convince him I would do just that. I told him I'd stop and I'd put your journal back." Lydia shrugged a shoulder as though what she was saying was nothing significant.

"I copied it and the next day, I slipped the USB drive and the phone into his luggage just in time for those goons you hired to get here and start searching people."

"He killed himself," PJ said, tears running down her face. Ellis may have been obsessed with PJ, and his spying had started all of this, but he didn't deserve to die.

Lydia laughed and the cruelty of it cut through PJ. "I know. It was beautiful, really. I couldn't have hoped for a better outcome. Icing on the cake, actually."

PJ heard the crack of her hand against Lydia's face before she realized she'd even moved. It was a stupid move with a gun in her side, but she hadn't actually planned to do it. When she heard the laughter and the callous words coming from the woman in front of her, she reacted without thought.

And then things happened so quickly, she couldn't really say what happened first or who moved when. Suddenly she was on the floor under Gabe and someone, maybe Justice, was tackling Lydia from behind. He'd come from the back of the bus in the split second following the slap.

But, the thing that registered most with PJ in that moment was the heat. The absolute, searing heat that ripped through her side. The pain that followed it was like nothing she'd ever felt before, and she fought to take a breath as she saw Justice and Eric secure a screeching Lydia.

Gabe's hands scrambled over her, tearing at her shirt while the door to their tour bus opened. She caught a glimpse of Debra and the police, and someone was calling for an ambulance and Gabe's hands pressed into her side.

"It just grazed you, Pru," he whispered to her, as the pain shot through her. It didn't feel like any graze to her.

What the hell did a real bullet wound feel like if this was what being grazed felt like?

Holy hell, there was a song in there somewhere, PJ thought, as Gabe pressed his lips to her temple and whispered in her ear while they waited for the ambulance.

"Been meaning to tell you," she said looking at his deep brown eyes. "I love you, Gabe Sawyer."

She didn't know what possessed her to say that now, but it seemed like a good time to get that out there. Before anything else happened.

He laughed. Well, that wasn't quite what she was going for, she thought with a frown. Not really what you want to hear when you say I love you for the first time.

But, he made up for it pretty quickly, pressing a kiss to her mouth just before the EMTs climbed onto the bus. "I love you, too, Prudence Jane. But, we'll have to talk about this later. They need to take you to the hospital now."

And, that was that. That was the first time her future husband told her he loved her. Hardly the thing great love songs are made of.

EPILOGUE

*P*J sighed as she crossed her legs under her on the couch, but it was a happy sigh. One of contentment and peace. After finishing out her tour and spending some time at her parents' house, she had moved into Gabe's Connecticut home with him and begun a life of normalcy and stability.

One with friends and a boyfriend she loved with all her heart. Trusted with the same.

She smiled as she lifted her guitar to her lap and listened to the music building in her mind. Her music had come back to her.

Only now she wrote only for herself. She no longer felt the pressure to create for the sake of an album or a tour. She could let the music flow through her and come at its own pace, in its own time.

She released songs for free on the Internet, and she performed occasional concerts with the proceeds going to organizations that help young mothers, or expecting teenagers who need support as they make decisions about their future.

PJ knew she'd been lucky to have her parents' support and unwavering love when she'd become pregnant at such a young age. Many girls weren't that blessed.

As she closed her eyes and began to play, the music flowed

through her into the guitar and lyrics began to form in her head. As with many of her songs lately, this one spoke of love so strong, it swept her world sideways and took her off her feet.

Of a life so filled with joy, she felt comfort and strength and peace in all she did. The words came effortlessly to her as the chorus began to play in her head before she even gave thought to what it should sound like. Her music had definitely returned.

~

Gabe watched in silence as Pru sang softly on the couch, her whole heart and soul wrapped in song, as he'd often seen her over the last few months.

She was barefoot, her hair still slightly damp from the shower, and she'd never looked more beautiful to him. He loved to watch her sing, to see her lose herself in complete contentment as music flowed from her. She sang of love and hope and a happiness she wished the world could share with her.

He dropped to his knees in front of her. He'd intended to wait until tomorrow night to do this. He had a fancy dinner planned. They'd eat out on the patio under the stars with candles and flowers and the quiet beat of the ocean behind them. But, he couldn't stop himself now.

Gabe pulled the box from his pocket as he watched a smile come over Pru and her song stopped. She blinked her eyes open and gasped when she saw him on his knees in front of her.

She was beautiful.

Love poured from her eyes, all for him, and he felt as though he might be able to rebuild his lost family after all. To find the home, the anchor, he'd always wanted. In her. She was it for him.

He should have better words for her. Something more eloquent. But, what came out instead was simply, "Be mine, Pru? Be my wife, my family, my love – forever?"

She was crying when she nodded, and he guessed she was as lost for words as he was. That was okay. They didn't need words.

As he pulled her into his arms and kissed her deeply, with all the love and passion he felt for her, he felt it coming back to him in waves. Their love was something so strong, so palpable, he felt it in everything they did, in every touch or thought they shared.

Gabe lifted her and carried her to the bedroom, where they both found ways to show their love to one another without the need for words. With only touch and taste, with gasps and moans, and pleasure unlike any he'd ever felt before Pru.

He was home. With her, wherever she went, he finally had a home.

PJ felt the warmth of Gabe's hand holding hers as they crossed the lawn to make their way to Jack and Kelly's house. She loved the feel of his hand around hers, so strong and steady. Always there for her. And now, she thought as she felt the ring he'd placed on her finger earlier—now, he would be hers forever.

Her parents had been thrilled when they'd called them earlier, and they promised to come for a visit soon to help her plan for the wedding. They would tell Gabe's mom when they visited her next week, provided she was having a lucid day.

As often as not, she was not aware of who they were when they visited, but with any luck, she'd be aware and happy for them when they saw her next. She'd been taking a new medicine that seemed to be bringing her more and more clear days.

They arrived a bit late, finding everyone else was already there. Out on the patio—watching Maddie and Ella play in the grass—sat Kelly, Samantha, Jill, and Jesse. Samantha was grinning and PJ listened to the conversation as she settled into a seat.

Gabe took off to join the other men who were hovering over a table where Mrs. Poole was unwrapping dishes. PJ didn't know how that woman kept up with feeding this group when they came over.

Jill rocked a car seat with one of their twins in it, though PJ couldn't say whether it was Nicholas or Mark. The other baby lay on a blanket next to Kelly, who was patting his back. Jill and Andrew had named the boys Nicholas Conner Weston and Mark Christopher Weston and they were adorable.

"We'll be releasing a new version next month to work out some bugs and add two new levels for the game," Samantha was saying and PJ knew she was talking about Tangled Legacy, the online game Sam had designed that was quickly taking on some of the biggest games in the industry.

Kelly beamed at Sam. "I'm so excited for you, Samantha! This is amazing."

Sam bit her lip. "I've got an offer from a company that wants to sell Tangled Legacy action figures and another one who wants to create a boardgame based on the game."

There was a lot of squealing to that and PJ couldn't help but grin as Samantha blushed. Samantha wasn't the kind of woman who loved attention, but she had to be feeling really good about what she'd accomplished. It wasn't the same kind of thing as PJ had gone through when she was discovered and her fame came hard and fast, but if Sam needed someone to talk to about that kind of life change, PJ would be there for her.

She looked at her friends and was grateful for the way her world had changed. If not for someone stealing her journal, she thought again.

She looked down at the now sleeping infant in the car seat.

"I swear, I think they get more beautiful each day," she said to Jill, who smiled back at her.

Jill looked tired, but there was likely nothing that could take that smile off her face. Even exhaustion. Motherhood looked so good on Jill, PJ began to wonder if she was ready to begin her own family now with Gabe. To have a baby she didn't have to give up.

A pang of guilt stabbed at her as she wondered how Matthew would feel if she had children of her own after giving him up, but she knew her aunt and uncle would help him get through it. They'd work through it together as a family.

Kelly leaned in and whispered to the group. "Don't look now, guys, but I think Mrs. Poole is finally giving into Roark."

They, of course, all turned at once making it more than obvious where they were looking. The couple standing by the table of food didn't seem to notice.

"What's that about?" PJ asked.

"That's Roark, Jack's lawyer," Kelly said. "He's a widow and he's been trying to get Mrs. Poole to go on a date with him for years."

"Years?" PJ asked, smiling as she looked at the older couple. Mrs. Poole was blushing, one hand resting on Roark's arm as he leaned in to say something to her.

"Years!" Kelly emphasized. "He took her out to dinner the other night and it was super cute. She was so nervous and he brought her flowers."

Jesse laughed. "It's weird that we call him Roark but we all still call Mrs. Poole Mrs. Poole."

Kelly laughed at that. "I know, right? I think I was living here a month before I even found out her first name. It's Greta, but she's always been Mrs. Poole."

"Let's hope that's not what Roark calls her in bed," Jesse said, earning an elbow from Kelly.

"PJ!" Jill said with a start, "What is that?"

PJ glanced down to her hand where Jill's round eyes were focused and where, thanks to Jill's not so subtle outburst, all eyes were now glued. PJ smiled at her friends, her heart kicking in her chest at the happiness that surrounded her.

"Gabe asked me to marry him," she said, her eyes finding Gabe's as the men approached.

They each leaned in to congratulate Gabe with one-armed hugs and manly slaps to his back, while the women surrounded her with hugs.

As PJ listened to the chatter of good friends around her, and watched as Kelly swung a laughing Maddie over her head and Jill and Andrew each patted a tiny baby's back, she knew she finally had everything she'd ever need in life.

A family, love, and good friends who would support her no matter the choices she'd made. She needed absolutely nothing else.

The End

Thank you so much for reading! Gabe and Pru were so fun to write and their story let me sink back into the Sutton family. One person whose story I've been DYING to write is Samantha. Listen, you know she needs a strong man, right? One who loves her quirks and accepts her for who she is. It turns out, her hero needs her just as much as she needs him. He's a Navy SEAL struggling to come home and settle back into a world he isn't sure he fits into anymore. And through all the sexy heartwarming moments, there's going to be a ton of heart-stopping action! I'll tell you a secret. This book is my favorite of all the books I've ever written. Like, EVER.

Grab The Billionaire's Navy SEAL here and binge now: loriryanromance.com/book/the-billionaire-and-the-navy-seal

Read on for chapter one of The Billionaire's Navy SEAL:

CHAPTER ONE

Logan Stone looked up when his boss—as of three hours ago—approached his office. Logan had been at his desk since five that morning but the time had gone by quickly with no distractions around to interrupt him.

He watched as Jack Sutton, CEO of Sutton Capital, entered the moderately-sized office with a large window on one wall, and sat in the chair across from Logan. He'd known Jack for a few months and respected the man as both the head of the company, and as a person.

Zach Harris, Logan's best friend and Jack's brother-in-law, was responsible for introducing the two men. Logan suspected Zach might be responsible for Jack giving him this job. A fact that grated on his nerves on a daily basis, but he needed the job. He wasn't exactly in a position to turn it down.

"Security told me you've been in the building since five," Jack said. "I gotta tell you, I do like hard workers, but you really don't need to be here that early."

Jack's smile was easy and his posture loose as he crossed one ankle over a knee. Logan wished he felt the same way, but edgy didn't even begin to describe what he was feeling.

Despite his mood, he grinned and shrugged, throwing a mask over his features. From what he'd heard, there was a time when Jack Sutton would have demanded his employees showed up earlier than the competition, and left later.

Being a husband and father had changed that in the last few years. Sutton Capital had been changing to a family-oriented company that prized relationships and quality of life as much as it valued dollars and cents. It still held a powerful position in the industry, but the environment of the company had changed dramatically in recent years.

"Wanted to get a jump on things." What the hell else could he say to explain his early arrival? No way would he tell Jack he'd made the twenty-minute drive to work at five in the morning because he wasn't yet able to drive in traffic. Because he needed the ability to run a red light when the panic set in. Because, most days, he had to roll through a stop sign and hope to avoid a ticket or worse if he was out when there weren't many people on the road.

Jack nodded as though he accepted the excuse and placed a stack of files on Logan's desk.

"These are the files I told you about. If you can go over them this morning, I'll tell Samantha to get with you this afternoon. You can run through your thoughts and get her perspective on things. She's familiar with all of the companies we're thinking of acquiring. She can often spot things I can't, so it's useful to touch base with her before we make any decisions."

Samantha Page. The woman had grabbed his attention at Zach's wedding three months ago. She was good friends with Zach's new bride, Jesse and with Jack's wife, Kelly.

Although he didn't talk to her directly the weekend of the destination wedding, he'd sure as hell noticed her. And damned if she hadn't been sauntering through his dreams every night since then. In fact, he owed her a debt there.

The one thing that had eased in the last three months since he'd medically retired from the military were his nightmares. He still had to deal with his memories when he was awake, but they didn't seem to come pounding on his door as often at night anymore. Sam had that distinction now.

Logan shoved aside thoughts of Sam with that long black hair and soft curves that plagued his dreams, and nodded. He pulled the files closer to him and scanned the names of the companies neatly typed on the edge of each one.

Jack had mentioned each of them in their prior talks and Logan already had a list of follow-up questions for Sam. Logan would be teaming up with three men and one woman who, like him, were new to Sutton Capital.

As someone who had been with Sutton Capital for years, Samantha would be his liaison to the rest of Sutton. She was set up to help get him and his team settled into the company and get up to speed on the companies Sutton Capital was interested in backing financially.

Logan's new team all had medical, science, or technology backgrounds—some earned in the military like him, one in a research firm he'd helped to found, and another as a physician.

He was glad Sam would be teaming up with him to lead the new team. From what he knew of her, she was a computer genius. She could hack just about anything you threw at her and had a deeper than average knowledge base of a hell of a lot of other topics as well. From what he'd heard from Zach, she was the kind of person who read physics textbooks for giggles as a kid, but she was cool enough to have designed a kickass online game that he had to admit, he'd spent many nights playing recently.

Sam's looks reminded him of one of those woman you might see painted on a plane in World War II. Back when women were real, with curves and full lips and a body a man could lose himself in. Not one of those damned french fry stick figures most women aspired to nowadays. Sam had curves and substance to her. Logan wouldn't feel like he might break her if he grabbed hold of her or tucked her up under him—

Hell.

"Logan?"

"Yeah?" The look on Jack's face told Logan his boss had been trying to get his attention without success.

"So, you're good to get with Sam at two?"

Get with Sam? Crap. Get it together, sailor.

"Sure." Logan picked up a pencil and jotted the notation on his desk planner. He was still old school in that respect, which some considered odd given his technology background. He liked a paper desk blotter with the calendar printed on it, and he still used the plain old yellow No. 2 pencils he'd learned to write with in elementary school.

Something about the graphite scratching across the paper settled him. People asked him how he could schedule appointments when he was away from his desk, but in reality, he didn't need to be near it. He could see the entire calendar in his head at any given moment. If he scheduled something while he wasn't in reach of the blotter, he simply wrote the notation in his head, imagining the feel and sound of the pencil as it left its markings on the page. That action alone was enough to embed the date and time so he could fill it in on the paper later.

Logan stood, needing to stretch his legs and move for a few minutes. "I'll walk with you," he said as Jack turned to leave. "I could use another cup of coffee."

In reality nothing could be further from the truth. His blood pressure was already pounding hot and heavy enough to meet the circulatory needs of a gorilla, but it was one more way to cover what was happening with his broken-ass body. The ache in his left hip and thigh got to be too great if he sat still for too long.

Broken body and broken mind. Two things he didn't want to share with anyone.

Samantha Page sipped the latte her friend had handed her and then smiled. She and Jennie Thompson stood shoulder to shoulder outside her office on the twenty-sixth floor of Sutton's office building. Her office was one of the twenty that ringed the outer edge of the room. The inner area of the large room held rows of cubicles and desks that she and Jennie looked out on now.

"No, I'm serious," she said eyeing Jennie, who was still laughing too hard to talk. "It's definitely time for a divorce. I'm just going to miss the ice cream."

Sam probably should have left out the ice cream bit. Jennie only laughed harder at that and it was clear she had more questions. Sam waited patiently while Jennie recovered.

She was used to people laughing at her, and to be truthful, with Jennie it always felt more like the old saying: Jennie was laughing with Sam, not at her. Sam could handle people laughing at her, though. Even by her friends. It happened. It didn't bother her anymore.

"What does divorcing your gym have to do with ice cream?" Jennie finally asked, using her fingertips to sweep an errant tear from under her eye.

Samantha shrugged a shoulder and grinned, knowing her workout routine wasn't exactly what most fitness gurus would recommend. In fact, even assigning the word "workout" to it was a bit of a stretch. Or fitness. Or routine, for that matter, since she didn't exactly go on a regular basis.

"If I finish whatever class I signed up for, I reward myself with an ice cream cone from the place next to the gym. If I started working out at home instead of the gym, I'd have to drive to get my ice cream cone and that just changes the whole thing. It's not as fun."

Jennie had been trying to convince Sam to hire a personal trainer. Sam's budget could definitely afford it, but frankly, she wasn't sure she wanted to pay someone to hound her to exercise. There would be no wheedling out of it if she wasn't in the mood, which, most of the time, she wasn't.

"And, tell me again why you have to *divorce* your gym?" Jennie emphasized the divorce part of the question, as if to stress how unusual it was to talk about divorcing a fitness center. Yeah, okay, so maybe that had been the wrong choice of words.

"It's got bad juju," Sam explained. "It's cursed. You can't deny the evidence. First, someone stole my wallet in the locker room the one time I forgot to bring my lock, then I ended up with a flat tire a week later, and yesterday someone sideswiped my car in the parking lot. They don't have cameras in the lot, so I'm screwed. I can get her repaired, but she'll never be the same."

Jennie nodded and sipped her drink. Everyone knew Sam's Jaguar was her baby. She didn't splurge on things often, but that car had been her one great splurge and she babied it. Coming out and seeing the scrapes and dents all along one side of Dahlia had made Sam want to cry. Or hit something. Or throw things. She'd actually done all of those things. And, stomped her feet.

"That is some bad juju. Maybe you could join another gym. Mine doesn't have an ice cream shop nearby, but there's a donut place."

"Ooooooo. Donuts could work." Her grin was wide, but the reason for her and Jennie's early arrival in the office walked through the door, distracting her from thoughts of food and workouts.

Three men and one woman followed the office's human resources director into the room.

The men looked like they belonged in a magazine or on the pages of a calendar. One of *those* calendars. And the woman looked to be five feet one or two inches of size-zero gorgeousness, designed to make other women feel inconsequential, at best.

"You have *got* to be freaking kidding me!" Samantha said, probably a little louder than she'd planned to.

She heard Jennie sputter and cough over a mouthful of latte and had to admit to a bit of chagrin when Jennie turned amused eyes on her.

"What?" Sam said defensively. "You're telling me you expected *that* for our new science and technology department? We should have gotten geeks and nerds, not underwear models and a woman who could easily pose for ... for ... for whatever the biggest fashion magazine is," Sam said with a glance to her own outfit.

Sam would have no fashionable clothes if it weren't for Jennie. When Sam's online game took off and she started earning more money than she knew what to do with, Jennie helped Sam trade in boxy business suits for cute skirts and blouses that accentuated Sam's curves. It had taken some talking to get Sam to see that, when showcased properly, her curves were beautiful.

And now Sam had a personal shopper who brought her clothes each month to choose from. She let Sam have her own unique style, as evidenced by the purple blouse and matching purple boots she wore today, which Sam loved.

Still, even with the personal shopper and help from her friends, Sam wasn't what one would consider a fashionista. Hence, her lack of knowledge about the titles of the latest and greatest fashion magazines.

Her friend shushed her and laughed as they watched the HR director continue her tour, the underwear models in question following her as the group made their way across the room.

"I'm just not sure I understand your issue with it, Sam. If I was going to be in charge of getting those guys settled into the company, I'm pretty sure I'd be psyched, not complaining. I mean, if I didn't have Chad, that is," Jennie said with a sly grin.

Jennie was happily married to Chad Thompson, head of Sutton Capital's security division and part owner in the company. Chad was also Jack's cousin and best friends with Andrew Weston, Sutton's Chief Financial Officer.

Chad, incidentally, was model-worthy himself. It didn't surprise Samantha that Jennie was married to such a good-looking man, since Jennie could also easily have landed the cover of Vogue or some swimsuit or underwear spread.

Samantha, on the other hand, was a normal person. She was one of those "average" females you heard about, who wore more than thimble-sized clothing. She was taller than the average woman at five foot eleven. Oh, Jennie told her differently.

Jennie said she was voluptuous and sexy, and Sam saw that to some extent. But she also faced reality. If she were a model, she'd be showing off sweatshirts and galoshes, not underwear.

"Why am I not happy about this?" Sam gestured to the men who stood in a loose circle across the room, each with the kind of easy confidence born of above-average looks and a physical fitness level that can only come from years of honing and driven attention to exercise. "Because we need some normal people around here."

Another coworker approached on Sam's side as she finished her sentence.

"Damn right we do," Tanya, the newcomer, said with a nod. Tanya worked in the finance department of Sutton and often had lunch with Jennie and Samantha.

"See, she gets it," Samantha said to Jennie, as she bumped her hip in solidarity against Tanya's, earning a smile from the other woman. "We're surrounded by above-average overachievers who look like they were crafted in the Ken and Barbie doll factory instead of a womb. We need average guys around here for those of us that weren't graced with those kind of genes," Sam said, casting a glance at Jennie. "No offense."

"Um, none taken. I think," Jennie answered with a huff of a laugh. "So you were hoping for ugly?"

"Not ugly. Just . . . normal. They're science geeks. I mean, come on. These people are supposed to be walking computers on everything from nanotech and biochemistry, to immunotherapy and whatever the hell else they do. They should, at the very least, be a little pale from being indoors too long, not tanned and glowing and all . . . all . . . "

"Godlike," Tanya finished for Sam.

"Yeah." Sam nodded. "Godlike. You'd think Jack would have given the teeniest bit of consideration to us mere mortals when he hired them. It's just selfish, is what it is. Selfish and inconsiderate. Just because Jack's all walking, talking sex-on-a-stick doesn't mean he shouldn't think of the rest of us once in a while. The guy could at least throw us a bone for once. Is that too much to ask?"

Sam looked at Tanya and grinned, expecting to find her coworker grinning back. Instead, Tanya looked past Sam and Jennie, her face a pale, pasty color—somewhat like the flour-and-water glue Samantha's mother used to make for her dioramas. In fact, she looked a bit like she might be sick.

Sam turned her head slowly, flinching the second she caught sight of her boss, the sex-on-a-stick man, in the flesh. Jack Sutton stood in the doorway of the office next to hers, another man next to him, both wearing expressions that clearly told her they'd heard every word she'd said.

Jennie only laughed, but given who her husband was, she could do that.

Sam heard Tanya squeak and mumble something about paperwork piling up. Sam knew if she turned, she'd see Tanya slinking back to her cubicle, where she'd no doubt crawl under her desk and hide.

But she didn't turn to check on Tanya. She was rooted to the spot, trying to figure out how to get her foot to either come back up her throat or go down smoothly. Her size nine, chunky-heeled, purple boot that she thought had looked so cute this morning was going nowhere. It was firmly lodged in her throat as a weird, choked sound eked out past it.

Before she could come up with words to try to cover her mortification, Jack grinned and gracefully let her off the hook.

"Jennie, Sam, have you met Logan Stone?"

Sigh. Had she met Logan Stone? No. She hadn't met him. She'd seen him, though. And drooled over him from across the room at her friend's wedding three months ago. And she'd dreamed about him.

She'd lusted after his dark eyes and the five o'clock shadow that graced a chiseled jaw and outlined a mouth she wanted to bite. Hair so dark it was almost black. Thick hair she wanted to pull as he, um ... so, yes, she'd dreamed about him. Hot, sweaty dreams that she'd prayed never to wake up from. In her dreams, they'd done a lot more than meet, going well past "hello, how are you" to "let me stick my tongue down your throat while we get started on our first-born child."

Somewhere in the back of Sam's mind, she knew running her gaze up and down the man's body was rude, but who could stop themselves?

He stood there all dark and scruffy in dark slacks and a charcoal sweater that hugged his biceps and chest. He looked photoshoot ready, and Sam had a hard time not being grateful that he wasn't covering himself up with a suit jacket.

She guessed going from BDUs and a flak jacket, or whatever it was SEALs wore, to a business suit was too much. She liked his choice of compromise just fine. She wondered briefly if spinning her finger in the air to indicate he should turn so she could see his backside would be too much.

Yeah. Probably. But maybe?

"Hi, Logan. It's so good to see you again," Jennie said smoothly, next to Samantha, putting her hand out to shake the man's. Samantha continued to stare.

Close your mouth.

Well, at least the voice in her head wasn't dumbstruck. That was always a positive.

On the negative side of the scale was the fact that Logan Stone had just heard her tirade against her boss's taste in men.

"And, this is Samantha Page," Jack said, gesturing to Sam as she forced her mouth to close. "She was going to be showing you guys the ropes and getting you settled in, but I think she's got some complaints to lodge with HR over your qualifications," Jack quipped and Sam found her mouth falling open once again.

He was joking about this? She'd called him sex-on-a-stick and he was joking?

Samantha closed her mouth and cleared her throat. "I'm good, Jack. No complaints here. I'll just, um, I'll get, um ...."

Oh, my hell. Stop babbling and say something—anything

—moderately intelligible. Or burst into flames. Developing the ability to go up in flames right now would be handy.

"Hi," the man of her dreams intoned, his deep voice washing over every atom of her body, stroking her in a way she'd felt only in her dreams. "It's nice to meet you, Samantha." He said the words, but kept his hands shoved in his pockets.

And, with that, in front of Jennie, her boss, and the man whose kids she hoped to have one day, Samantha Page opened her mouth and said, "Gah."

～

Logan knocked on the jamb of the open door to Sam's office. He'd spent the rest of the morning in meetings with his new team and Jack. They prioritized the research projects Jack wanted everyone working on and the acquisitions Logan would be looking into in the coming months.

"Hey, Sam." Logan watched as Sam's head shot up, her attention ripped from her computer, which apparently held something enthralling. So enthralling, she hadn't noticed he'd been watching her for the past few minutes. The woman intrigued the crap out of him. Unfortunately.

She had a habit of rubbing the tip of her nose with her index finger as she focused, then tapping it whenever she smiled as though she'd had a breakthrough or some big "aha!" moment.

Logan blinked his eyes purposely, a trick he'd used during his years in special ops when he needed to clear his mind and refocus. Like the click of an old slide show projector, Logan moved to the next frame in his mind.

He focused solely on Samantha as a co-worker, not as an erotically tantalizing woman with a kick-ass body he'd love to get his hands on. It was an exercise he'd be doing a lot of, if they were going to work together.

He had no business getting involved with anyone with the

state his head was in. He needed to focus on planting one foot in front of the other, right now. On just making sure he made it through the day without losing the shit that seemed to be swimming around in his head for brains nowadays. There wasn't time for anything other than that, and sure as hell not with a woman like Sam.

"Jack told me to come see you at two. He said you've done some of the preliminary work for us on a few of the companies he wants to look into," Logan said, a little intrigued with the way she openly ogled him from head to toe.

She didn't even seem to realize she was doing it. It was almost comical how blatantly she allowed her eyes to skim him from head to toe. If it wasn't so comical, he might squirm under the scrutiny, but nothing about her gaze made him uneasy.

"Sam?" he prompted when she still hadn't answered him.

"Hmmm? Oh! Lunch."

"What?" He didn't know what she meant. He hadn't mentioned lunch and it was already two o'clock.

Her eyes cut to the small clock that sat on the corner of her desk and he heard her murmur quietly about it being lunchtime already. He wondered how often she forgot to eat when she was into something. And how often she talked to herself, even when there was someone else in the room.

"Uh," she said almost distractedly as she leaned over and used her mouse to save something on the screen before locking the computer. "I need to go eat lunch. Come with me and we'll talk while we eat?" She picked up her purse and faced him.

"Uh." Real suave, idiot. How to explain that he brought lunch so he wouldn't have to leave the building? "I, uh already ate."

"No biggie," she said, seemingly unfazed. "You can have dessert." She walked to the office door as though she expected him to follow her, and follow he did. Like a freaking puppy. What the hell was wrong with him?

As they stood by the elevator, Sam cocked her head to one

side, her expression thoughtful. As he waited to see what she'd do, trying to decipher the maddening scent that had to be a pheromone of some sort, he noted she was even taller than he'd thought. She must be close to six feet tall.

So close to his own six feet two inches in those boots, he wouldn't even have to duck his head to close the space between them and taste those full lips of hers. He imagined they'd taste like cherries or strawberries, but that was probably only because of the berry red lipstick she wore.

He didn't expect it at all when Samantha reached a hand out and squeezed his bicep. Her hand felt too damned good over the cotton of his shirt. She ran her hand up to his shoulder, her fingertips grazing lightly over his collarbone. Hell, if that didn't send a message straight to his groin. The expression on her face was almost analytical in its intensity. Her touch was clinical, but his body didn't seem to give a damn.

Great. A hard-on at the office on his first day. What a proud moment.

"Hmm. It really is just like a romance novel." She left the odd statement out there and turned to enter the opening elevator doors, as though she hadn't just felt him up.

Logan felt a grin on his face and another laugh he hadn't expected bubbling up in his chest. Luckily, the strange way her mind worked intrigued him enough that his dick started to settle down in his pants and he was able to follow her.

Catching up, he let one hand fall to her elbow for no other reason than he wanted more contact with her. He leaned in close. "What's like a romance novel?"

Samantha froze and turned round eyes on him. "Damn, I said that out loud? Have to stop doing that," she seemed to admonish herself, stabbing the button marked L for Lobby in brass letters.

"Did I—" she cut herself off as she glanced at his shoulders.

He laughed. "Feel me up? Yes. That wasn't happening in your head, either."

Logan put his back against the wall and turned to face the double doors. Standing shoulder to shoulder, she turned to him with one of the most earnest expressions he'd ever seen.

"I apologize. I don't have an internal filter. I'm the only one in my family who was born without one. It used to embarrass the heck out of my sisters. I always said the wrong thing in front of their boyfriends. I never fit in at school. I would have been a total pariah if it weren't for my sisters and brothers paving the way for me." Samantha sighed and he bit back a grin. "Anyway, I just never managed to grow a filter so you'll have to excuse my random babbling from time to time."

Logan felt the corners of his mouth twitch as he nodded. "Got it. No problem. Ignore random babbling."

The hell he would. He loved the random things she said. They were funny, and when she combined them with actually reaching out and feeling him up? He could get on board with that in a heartbeat.

Logan held the elevator door open when they landed in the lobby. The crowd of people moving in and out of the four units that made up the elevator bank of the large building kicked an unwelcome agitation into high gear. He gritted his teeth as they moved through the crowd and tried to get Samantha to begin babbling again.

"How many sisters and brothers do you have?"

"Three older sisters and two older brothers." Her smile was wide as she answered.

"The baby then, huh?"

"Yup. And, they never let me forget it."

Logan paused when they hit the sidewalk and looked in both directions. To an outsider, he probably looked undecided about where to go. He stretched his neck, tilting his head from side to side, attempting to relieve the strain tightening his muscles. The back of his neck always felt like chunks of calcite were grating into each other in there. Always grating and grinding, setting his teeth on edge.

"What's good around here?" Logan turned to Sam as he spoke and noticed her studying him.

Sam nodded to a place across the street to the right. "I usually go to the bagel place. They have sandwiches and great coffee and they also serve breakfast all day if you want it. Or there's a Mexican place farther up the street. When it gets warmer out, make sure you try the Thai cart that parks across the street. They have really fantastic Pad Thai, but they won't show up for another few weeks."

Logan nodded. "Bagels work." They stood side by side near the crosswalk, waiting for the light to change. Logan edged his way to the back of the small group of people waiting there and let his eyes roam.

A crushed soda can lay in the gutter only feet from them. A parked car sat three yards down. A van idled beside it, double parked with no driver in sight. Logan took another step backward and shot a glance to the light. Still no sign of the little lighted man that would tell them to cross. His fists clenched and unclenched and he realized he had fallen into the patterned combat breathing that had become a way of life out on an op.

Lost in the moment, he was shocked when Sam put her hand in his. She pulled him several yards back, toward the edge of the building, away from the crowd and the cars.

"I prefer to wait in the shade," she said simply, letting go of his hand and turning to watch the light at the corner. She studiously avoided his gaze.

Shade, my ass. It was in the forties and, if not cloudy, certainly not sunny by any means. Although he hated that she might have noticed his tension, he felt the tightness in his chest ease.

It was a little thing, waiting that short distance away, but having his back to the building and just a bit of space gave him back the ability to breathe. He was able to think clearly and rationally instead of listening to the screeching alarm bells in his head. And, he had a feeling she knew exactly what she was doing, but wasn't going to make a big deal of it.

Logan glanced down at her again as the light changed and they took off toward the bagel place, crossing the street just a little behind the crowd. They were quiet while ordering their food at the walk-up counter, but Logan picked up the subject of family again when they found seats near the back of the restaurant. Sam nodded and followed him when he pointed to the booth against the wall.

"So, is your family nearby?" he asked. The restaurant was on a corner, with two entrances, one on either of the facing streets. He popped the top on his bottled iced tea and took a large gulp, letting his gaze take in the people surrounding them.

A family with two young kids at the table next to them; four men in suits on the other side; a few tables with only one person, all looking like they came from the surrounding office buildings. Two police officers in uniforms in the far corner.

From his position, Logan could watch the two doors, but he wasn't so close to either entrance that people caught him off guard when opening the door. As Samantha began to talk, he found the churning in his gut slowing. He could almost pretend he was normal in her presence. She sure as hell did a good job of acting like he was, even though he was pretty sure nothing was getting by her.

Sam nodded. "My parents are in Massachusetts, an easy drive on the weekends, and most of my siblings are spread out in this area. Two in New York City, another in New Jersey, and two in Philly."

"So you guys are all close?"

She gave a funny tilt of her head back and forth and a little shrug of a shoulder. "As close as one can be to a family of jocks and prom queens when you skipped three grades and were more focused on writing code than you were on fitting in."

Logan raised an eyebrow. "You hardly seem like a black sheep."

She shrugged a shoulder again, mumbled something about not quite fitting the mold and quickly changed the subject. He let her.

"What about you? Do you have family nearby?"

Logan shook his head no. "Only my dad and he's up in New Hampshire."

"No sisters and brothers?"

"Nope."

There was an uncomfortable lull and he felt like a jackass for being so short. Family wasn't something he had fond memories of. His dad was an alcoholic who served as little more than an embarrassment to Logan growing up. They didn't have a relationship. After Logan's mother had died when he was seven, he'd essentially raised himself.

Logan had been a bit of an outcast in school as well. He was more into computers and books than a lot of the kids in his school, and he'd been scrawny growing up.

When he'd started getting his ass kicked on the playground every day, he'd signed himself up for karate lessons. And that was how he and Zach met and became best friends. Zach was a brother to him now. They'd taken care of each other. Still did.

Sam cut into his thoughts, and into the stiff silence. "So, Jack has you looking at Kleintech? Is he thinking of pulling the plug on their funding?"

"Maybe not pulling it altogether, but at least sending some of us in to oversee things for a while. It looks like Arty Klein is a brilliant scientist, but not exactly a crack businessman. Jack is pretty sure if we straighten things out on the business side, the technology is still worth the investment. I'm planning to send Jaxon down there next week so he can go over the books and streamline things."

"Jaxon Cutter." She looked like she was running through a

computer in her head, and from what he'd heard about Sam from Jack and Zach, that made sense. If what they'd told him was true, Sam was easily the smartest woman he'd ever met and he'd worked with some crazy intelligent women in the military.

Sam could hack just about any program and he wouldn't be surprised to hear she had an eidetic memory.

She began to spout off what sounded like a summary of Jaxon's military service record. "Honorable discharge two years ago, Navy Corpsman to the Marines, a couple of bullets took his spleen, a piece of one lung, and his left leg below the knee. A lot of his record is redacted. I thought about hacking it, but Jennie has told me I shouldn't dig into the personal lives of people I know. Apparently, it's rude."

Logan found himself squirming now, realizing Sam had probably read about each of his injuries as well. She might even be aware of the struggle he had even walking some days, after having taken a hell of a lot of shrapnel to his thigh and hip.

Luckily, their food arrived, providing a reprieve. He dug into the chips that filled one half of the green basket set in front of him. Logan steered the conversation back to work for the rest of the half hour and Samantha treated him to more of her "unfiltered" thoughts, including her musings as to whether Jack would be firing her after overhearing her rant that morning.

Logan had to grin at that. He'd heard stories about Sam from Zach long before he saw her at the wedding. Maybe that was why she'd fascinated him so completely right off the bat? Because he'd built her up in his mind over the years.

Sam had been instrumental in rescuing Jack's wife, Kelly, from human traffickers intent on auctioning her off. Logan was fairly sure that involvement meant no one at Sutton had the authority to fire Sam. Not even Jack Sutton himself.

Logan was quiet as he watched her eat the apple pie she ordered with her sandwich. He hadn't taken her advice of having dessert, opting to have a second lunch instead. She had been right about the sandwiches. The place was good. But watching her eat the gooey confection in front of her made him want dessert.

Or her. One or the other. Or both. One on top of the other.

Ugh.

He cleared his throat, searching for some topic to clear his head. "Corpsmen are some serious shit. After everyone else is sitting down catching some Zs or eating, they're still going around checking everyone, patching shit up. They've got stamina like you wouldn't believe. Guts to match." He'd known some amazing Corpsmen during his time overseas. Respected the hell out of all of them.

Sam nodded, her brows knit together. "It's hard to imagine what it's like to be in a war zone, having never gone through it, you know?"

They were quiet again, but it wasn't uncomfortable. Just thoughtful.

"How did you know what to do back there? When you pulled me away from the crosswalk?" Logan didn't know where the question had come from.

The nagging sense that she'd known exactly what he was struggling with while waiting for the light hadn't left him since they sat down. He didn't know how he felt about it.

In some ways, he was grateful she'd snapped him out of his own head. In other ways, it disturbed the hell out of him that she'd seen through him so quickly. He'd thought he was doing a better job of hiding things. And, the thought that others might catch on set his neck muscles to gnashing again.

"Um ..." Samantha squirmed in her seat.

He couldn't help but laugh. Why would she feel weird about it? He should be the one feeling uncomfortable in this conversation. And yet, here she was once again, setting him at ease with something he sure as hell shouldn't be comfortable with.

"I don't really do well in relationships. Oh, wait! I don't mean that *that* way. I didn't mean to say we're in a relationship, because obviously we're not." As he watched, her face blushed a furious red and she began to wave her hands in front of her as though she were trying to erase what she'd just said. "I mean, we work together. Not that I wouldn't want a relationship with you. You're hot. I mean, really truly hot. So, don't be offended. I just meant relationship in the sense that I don't relate well to people all the time. Not relationship like dating. I mean people think I'm weird and they don't always get me and I don't always get people or, well ..."

Logan took pity on her. "Sam."

"Huh?" She looked up at him, doe eyes huge.

"Stop. I get it."

"Oh. Okay." She nodded and took a deep breath. "So anyway, I don't always get relationships and people and stuff. So, when Jack said some of you had a military background, I researched returning vets. I thought I could see what issues veterans deal with when they come back to the States. I found a lot of websites that talk about the kind of stuff you guys go through, so I could relate to what you were feeling. Only I don't think I actually can. Not that I don't want to, but I mean really, who can relate to a thing like war, unless you've lived in it? Right?"

Now, he did squirm.

"Oh! But, you don't want to talk about that, right? Daisies."

"What?"

"Daisies. I just planted daisies in a pot in my window. I'm not sure if they're going to grow or not. I think I got them in early enough, but I'm not really great with plants. I mean, I get all the theory of them. I can look up all the information and follow the directions, but I don't always seem to be able to apply all the information and get results, you know?"

Logan nodded as he realized she was changing the subject and letting him off the hook. The result was a little mind-spinning as she launched into a lecture of the dos and don'ts of growing daisies in a pot, in the window.

He had to admit, it helped. And, he couldn't help but wonder at her assessment that she sucked at relationships and reading people. She seemed to be damned good at knowing exactly when he needed her to move on, and she did it. No questions asked. She might move on to some strange topic, like the care and growth of daisies, but she did it. He had a feeling she was a lot better with people than she realized.

Get The Billionaire's Navy SEAL here: loriryanromance.com/book/the-billionaire-and-the-navy-seal

ABOUT THE AUTHOR

Lori Ryan is a NY Times and USA Today bestselling author who writes romantic suspense, contemporary romance, and sports romance. She lives with an extremely understanding husband, three wonderful children, and two mostly-behaved dogs in Austin, Texas. It's a bit of a zoo, but she wouldn't change a thing.

Lori published her first novel in April of 2013 and hasn't looked back since then. She loves to connect with her readers.

For new release info and bonus content, join her newsletter here.

Follow her online:

facebook.com/loriryanromance
twitter.com/Loriryanauthor
instagram.com/loriryanauthor

Made in the USA
Columbia, SC
22 April 2021

36709423R00121